THE NONESSENTIALS II

Z. MARTIN BROWN

Pathogen Press

THE
NONESSENTIALS

"The only difference between me and a madman
is that I'm not mad."

— Salvador Dali

To my mother,
who's always encouraged me to chase my dreams

1. FLEETING, MAGICAL MOMENTS

THE NIGHTMARE IS OVER. THAT'S WHAT I'VE been repeating inside my head as I lie awake, waiting for my graveyard shift to end, for the last seven hours, twenty-six minutes, and eighteen seconds—but who's counting? Me, Max, that's who.

Sleep has been a losing battle for weeks, thanks to my night terrors. I'm exhausted, and likely depressed too, but who isn't these days? Not to mention, I feel ashamed for what I'm about to admit. I swore to the closest people in my life that I don't need it anymore, but I'm not there. ... I need a fix.

I've been trying to cope without copping out. For one thing, I put the kibosh on talking to reporters. Retelling the story of how my friends and I saved Washington State from becoming a mass grave wasn't doing me any good, especially with some of the gruesome details.

I'll spare you the worst of those for now. Let's just say that many innocent people died and even more people got hurt, all thanks to a few assholes: local pigs, a corrupt and powerful family, and that twisted-fuck funeral home director ... Jim. That bastard killed my mother, and now he's driving around in my Beast.

Since then, the media has treated me like a hero, but it sure doesn't feel good to be one. I'm trying to move on, to stop obsessing about the things that I can't change. I've cut myself off from the world for now, avoiding all media—TV, radio, newspapers, you name it. I've even removed YouTube from my phone. My algorithm was flooding me daily with fear-mongering clickbait:

"Millions Will Lose Everything If This Bill Passes!"

"You're Being Lied To! Join Us This Full Moon To Find Out The Truth!"

"You're Probably Using THIS Common Product That Could Be Killing You!"

I need to focus on other news, real news, the kind that matters. Like that Carter's broken ribs are almost as good as new, and Chuck is healing slowly but surely.

Crutch, Sunshine, and I have been working around the clock to help those two with their recovery. It was Sunshine's idea for us to work individual eight-hour shifts, instead of crowding the house with all of us simultaneously.

"We'll split up the day into thirds," she explained to Crutch and me. "That will give us all personal time and space. We can share notes in a logbook."

Sunshine, as a morning person, opted for the early shift from seven to three. Crutch volunteered for the second leg, and I didn't mind taking the late shift. Staying up with the stars is nothing new for me. It was my usual routine back when I ran my light therapy clinic in Bellingham. I often kept Brighter Days open until well past three, sometimes even five in the morning.

I consider myself a rational person, or at least, I try to be, and I realize that taking shifts makes sense. Split up the day—sure, why wouldn't we? But selfishly speaking, I wish we were working together. I would get to spend more time with, well ... her—Sunshine. I just can't shake this high school crush.

It's not like I don't get to see her. We talk every day at the end of my shift, and although all we seem to chat about are medical updates, those moments are now the brightest part of my days.

Each morning, at seven o'clock on the dot as if time's on a loop, my ears perk up at the squeal of brakes and an engine sputtering to a stop. *She's here!* I raise my head from the living room sofa, reach over to the window, and bend the blinds to peer outside.

I watch her hop out from the driver's seat of the Jeep and make her way toward the front door. Seeing her in the daylight makes the loneliness of each sleepless night bearable. To close my eyes for even a millisecond would mean missing these fleeting, magical moments.

Still, I need a fix.

2. A GODSEND, A SAVAGE

MY BURNER PHONE RINGS INSIDE THE BREAST pocket of my black blazer. I lift it, and across its monochromatic screen I read: *Unknown Caller.* Now, I've been waiting for a call. Hell, I've been expecting a certain someone to ring me for days. But I don't press the *TALK* button. Not just yet. My superb survival instinct tells me: *Jim, you handsome devil, let it go to voicemail instead.*

I have a damn good reason to be cautious. I'm currently a free man, but I'm also a desired man—wanted by the FBI. I must keep a low profile. Even where I sit now, enclosed in the cab of my Meat Wagon behind some Walgreens outside of bum-fuck-nowhere, Nevada late at night, I can't be too careful.

There's no room for mistakes. I've got hundreds of miles of road ahead and a fuck-load to accomplish in a brief fucking time. Above, the moon is waxing, and when it enters its fullest phase, so will Project Exodus—a magnificent endeavor, the likes of which the world has never seen!

And who better to lead such a project than me, Jim? Goddamn right. I'm the most charming motherfucker on either side of the Mississippi. I'm a godsend, a savage warrior always five steps ahead of the competition, and nobody can take that away from me!

Jim! JIM! JIM!!!

And just like that, my paranoia retracts into that ice-cold and unforgiving abyss inside me, like an ocean wave vanishing back to the sea after crashing on the shore.

That's better. I needed that pep talk. Now, where was I?

Oh yes. My phone is ringing.

3. Underneath my Facade

SCREEEECH!

The familiar pitch of the Jeep's brakes rouses me from my half-asleep, half-awake state, and as if hypnotized, I find myself cracking the blinds and peering out.

Sunshine steps out from the Jeep and strolls toward the house, carrying a box from Larry's Donut Shop. I wave at her, beaming like an idiot. She notices me at the window and sheds a warm smile that lifts her from the three-dimensional plane, making her four.

I speed toward the entrance and thrust the door wide open just as Sunshine reaches it. "It's nice to see you," I whisper. "Our patients are still sleeping."

"Nice to see you too, Max," she whispers back. She enters and sets her load on the coffee table.

I sink back onto the sofa, but she remains standing. I realize that the cushions are buried under my pillows and rumpled blankets, reeking of stale sweat from another restless night. Embarrassed, I sweep off my bedding and toss it onto the La-Z-Boy in the corner. She smiles and sits on the opposite end of the sofa.

"Sorry about that," I tell her.

"No worries. Help yourself," Sunshine says, pointing at the doughnut box. I thank her, then grab a maple bar and shove it in my mouth. "So, how did your night go?" she asks—of course, the second I chomp down on a giant chunk of dough.

I chew as fast as humanly possible. She stares at me, waiting for a response, but all I can do is smack my lips and hold up a finger to signal *one minute, please.*

How embarrassing would it be if I began to choke? *Don't choke, Max, chew.* Chew, and don't you dare think about how over five thousand people choke to death each year in the U.S. alone.

Like a sick joke, the faster I grind my choppers, the more the dough seems to expand inside my mouth. Quick-growing saliva-activated doughnuts—ha!

Finally, the goo-ball slides down my throat and into my gullet. Sunshine's still looking at me. "Yes, my night," I stall. Damn you brain, get your ass in gear. I need you now, so work with me! Sadly, my brain is comatose from lack of sleep.

All I can come up with is: "Well, Chuck was in the crapper most of the night. I heard the toilet flush six times." Talk about the most unromantic conversation in the world. The mere mental image of Chuck taking a shit is terrifying.

Sunshine nods. "Interesting ... I'll see if anyone at the hospital has some advice." She leans over the coffee table and lifts the notepad we've been using as a medical logbook. She scribbles into it, then asks, "Uncle Chuck's been drinking his herbal tea and taking his pills, right?"

The tea is a mixture of peppermint leaves for upset stomachs and chamomile to help him sleep through the night. The pills are supposed to help prevent infection from his liver and ankle surgeries.

"He did mention that he can't stand the taste of the tea," I tell her. "Something about peppermint and how it makes him gag. As for his pills, he tells me he takes two every night."

And just like yesterday, and the day before, our conversation becomes business—nothing close to the witty, flirtatious dialogue of a rom-com.

Sunshine jots down some notes, her pen scratching furiously across the paper. "I see ... I'll make some adjustments to the tea. What else?"

"Well, I noticed we're almost out of gauze."

"Seriously?" she asks, twisting her head in my direction. "I thought we had a few boxes left. How often have you been changing it out?"

"Me? He told me you were doing it, and he didn't need my help anymore." I hadn't been sure I believed him, but I would never dare to argue with the big guy.

"What? He told me you were changing it."

"Well, he's either doing it himself, or maybe Crutch is helping him. Whatever the case, he's been going through gauze like toilet paper at a county fair after a chili cook-off," I say. Then I add without thinking, "Well, hopefully not like Anderson Mill toilet paper!"

It's a dumb joke, and a hugely thoughtless one, and I realize it as soon as I see the pained expression on Sunshine's face.

"Got it." Sunshine's voice is a monotone. "Well, Max, I'll see about switching Chuck to a tea without peppermint. And after my shift at St. Joseph, I'll pick up a few more boxes of gauze."

It's quiet. I'm just bobbing my head and feeling stupid because I know why she sounds irritated. I'm an asshole for bringing up the Anderson Paper Mill. In the recent fiasco, Sunshine was kidnapped and forced to assist in a diabolical organ harvest operation, and it all began with corporate greed and poisoned paper products from that mill.

Each day after her shift, Sunshine commutes straight to St. Joseph Medical Hospital in Bellingham. She's been volunteering her spare time there for weeks, cleaning rooms and taking care of patients, even sleeping in a spare hospital bed. She says she loves it there, but there's more to it than that. She's haunted by having been part of something so evil.

I've told her, "Sunshine, you were chipped. Your mind was controlled. It wasn't your fault!" But she just turned away, saying, "It doesn't matter, Max, it's the least I can do." Hell, who am I to tell someone how to make peace with their conscience?

So we don't talk about the recent past much. Unfortunately, there's not much else we have in common to talk about. We didn't interact much in high school, since she was older and ran with a more popular crowd. And these days, we've been fixated on the condition of Chuck and Carter, how they're reacting to their medications, the supplies they need, and so on. Our talks have become crystallized inside these topics that have nothing to do with us.

An awkward silence stifles the room. I've been waiting for the perfect time to ask her anything besides the usual clinical chit-chat. But this perfect moment I'm hoping for will never happen —so fuck it, why not break the cycle today and ask her something simple about herself? Something personal, an ice-breaker that might lead to a real, meaningful conversation?

I can do this. I can talk to her.

I blurt out, "How's your hospital bed?"

Her face turns sour, and a wrinkle creases her forehead. "It's not the best," she says.

Max, you spectacular idiot. I know what a hospital bed feels like; it's a glorified gurney, stiff and narrow. Why would anyone want to talk about their unfortunate sleeping arrangements? What if she'd asked me, how's Chuck's lousy sofa? *How's your hospital bed?* I replay my foolish question inside my thick head, hearing how stupid I must have sounded. *How's your hospital bed—How's your hospital bed*—say something else, quick!

"That ... sorry—bed, bad?" Damnit! Now I sound like I'm having a stroke.

She's quiet; maybe she didn't hear me. I keep my mouth shut, not trusting my tongue to work. A moment later, she says, "Max, I've been meaning to ask ..."

My heart skips a beat. "Yes? What is it?" I sit there sweating, waiting for her question.

"How have you been?"

I'm floored. A personal question. Sunshine beat me to the punch.

How am I?

Where do I even begin? Well, I'm sure what she'd like to hear is that I'm super-duper awesome right now. That I'm a stronger, better version of myself: Max 2.0. Telling her this might make her laugh, and that too is what every girl wants, right? A strong and funny guy—some buff comic stud-muffin who could arm curl her while standing on hot coals, right?

How am I?

Should I be honest with her? Do I tell her that I feel like a tiny gnat in a tornado, a bug caught in an endless cycle of fear and soul-crushing anxiety? Is that what she wants to hear? About my insomnia? About the years I've spent dwelling on how we're all going to end up six feet under? Do I tell her that I obsess over how my existence is temporary, and I can't understand why everyone isn't panicking all the time? Why it's only me who can't shake these thoughts?

How am I?

Should I mention that looping in my head is a never-ending primal scream of thoughts that read like a transcript from the wrong end of a mental-help hotline?

Should I tell her I'd chop off my little toe for twenty minutes inside one of my light therapy booths, soaking up that soothing magenta glow? How much I crave that fix?

Hold up, Max. She doesn't want to hear any of this. Who in the hell would want to listen to your sob story?

My Problems, by Max Maddison.

Yeah, fucking right.

"I'm fine," is all I dare to say.

"You're still okay with this arrangement, you know, being here every night?" Sunshine asks. "It must be tough on you."

"Don't worry about me," I tell her. "There's already two people in this house to worry about. I promised Chuck and Carter I'd be here for them, no matter how long it takes them to get back on their feet."

Sunshine stares at me, and I feel like she's somehow digging deep into my brain. As if she knows that there is something else, a hidden truth underneath my facade. *Can she read minds?*

I shrug. "Anyway, what else would I do? It's not like I've got a job to return to."

It's true. My therapy lights are locked up with the FBI, and yes, it was me who told them, "Keep them as long as you like," so the government is doing just that. Stupid me.

"Speaking of your old job ... you don't need your ... you know?" Sunshine trails off.

"A fix? No way. No more magenta lights for me, I'm cured."

As soon as the lie escapes my mouth, I feel like shit. I try to play it off by smiling, but my lips won't cooperate, and now I look guilty as fuck.

Maybe I should tell her what's on my mind. Maybe I'm playing this tough-guy thing all wrong. It's not too late to come clean. I let out a sigh. "Well ... to tell you the truth, Sunshine—"

"Guys! You're not going to believe this!" Carter yells. We turn our heads and see him racing toward us from down the hall. He's breathing hard with one hand clutching his bandaged ribs, the other brandishing his phone above his head. He skids to a stop in front of us.

"Fucking hell!" Carter shouts. "How can you two just be sitting there like a couple of idiots?"

"Hey, take it easy," I tell him.

"What are you talking about?" Sunshine asks, sounding irritated.

Carter tosses his phone to his cousin, and she pulls the screen close to her face. As she reads, her eyelids flutter and her hands begin to shake.

"What ... what is it?" I ask.

"Here," she says, trying to hand me the phone.

"Just tell me! What is it?"

She shakes her head and shoves the phone toward me again. This time, I yank it from her grip and stare at the screen. I can't believe what I'm reading. It's an article published today by the Seattle Times with the headline: *Another Deadly Outbreak Hits Seattle's Streets!*

Suddenly I'm a child again, staring at my grandfather's waxen face in his casket. My mother crouches beside me, whispering in my ear:

"We're all going to die, sweetie. Everyone will end up six feet underground!"

4. Less-than-ideal Nature

My phone won't stop ringing: *Unknown Caller*. With a sigh, I press the green TALK button on my burner phone and shove it against my ear.

Static spews from the speaker for a moment. Then a robotic voice says, "Hello, you have a prepaid call from ... Holtz ... an inmate at Federal Detention Center SeaTac. This call is subject to recording and monitoring. To accept this call, press One. To refuse this call, hang up now. If you would like to permanently block your number from receiving calls from the Federal Detention Center SeaTac, press Nine."

My finger hovers over button Nine for a moment. With a sigh, I press button One. After a brief pause, Holtz's voice comes through the line: "Are you there?"

"Yes, Mr. Holtz. I'm here. How are you holding up?"

"Holding up? How's this for holding up? The judge denied my bail even though I need an operation, my cellmate has horrible sleep apnea, and to top it off, I haven't had a decent cup of coffee in weeks! I'm dying here. Holding up? Christ, cut the shit. Why the hell are my wife and I still in cages?"

"Err, well ..."

There was a little snag, I want to say, but that's an understatement. There have been many snags, and they haven't been little.

First of all, the FBI has had a hard-on for me since I've been on the move. They're on the lookout for a middle-aged, ridiculously handsome man (me), Dr. Howson, and a behemoth with no-neck—Junior. If you haven't seen Junior before, let me tell you, that son-of-a-fuck does *not* blend. He's a freak of nature, built like a brick house. So we had to split up to avoid being recognized together.

The next hiccup was a police chase and subsequent collision with a tree. Then our precious patient almost kicked the bucket, which led to Doc almost getting nabbed while stealing medical equipment from a clinic. Excuse my French, but I can't fucking wait until this leg of the job is in the rearview fucking mirror.

"Mr. Holtz, we ran into a minor dilemma, but we—"

"A dilemma? Christ! Always something with you, isn't it? One pathetic justification after another. You better wish on a fucking star that this *dilemma* is minor! Maybe I made a blunder by keeping you on my team. You with your empty promises. Fuck! Look at this despicable disarray—this filth you've made. And after everything my wife and I have done for you, or have you forgotten? Not so long ago, you were a heartbroken spineless worm, a penniless divorced schmuck—remember how your ex-wife treated you? Who plucked you from the burning ashes and gave you a second chance at life? Tell me, who helped you? *Who?*"

"You did, sir."

"You're damn fucking right I did!"

I take in a king-size breath before I say soothingly, "Mr. Holtz, sir, I'm grateful, always have been, and I'm aware of the less-than-ideal nature of your situation. But I assure you, sir, there's no reason to be alarmed."

"No reason? I can give you a thousand fucking —" His rant is cut short by violent hacking.

"Sir, are you okay?"

"Am I okay? No! I'm dying, you dipshit."

"Mr. Holtz, don't worry about a thing. Junior is on his way to you—"

"Junior? Shit, man, that's all you had to say. When?"

"Soon, sir. Before the full—"

A robotic voice cuts in. "Your call has ended due to insufficient funds. Goodbye." Beep.

Shit. That's that. Well, I still have a job to finish. "Samantha!"

Through the speakers of my meat wagon, Samantha says crisply, "Yes, Jim. How may I assist you?"

"Map me the fuck out of here! Fastest route to our future headquarters, got me?"

"Certainly, Jim." A digital map appears on the dash. "Twelve hours and forty minutes to Snake Bend, Arizona, sir. I included the necessary stops for fuel and provisions."

God, I love her. "Fan-fuckin'-tastic, Samantha. Now tell me, have our essentials RSVP'd for our upcoming event?"

"Yes, Jim. Many are scheduled to arrive soon after we do."

"And you messaged our friend the address?"

"Yes, Jim. 994 East Winston Street, Deming, Washington."

"Samantha, if I could kiss you, I would. Now, tell me, is there any news about me today?" I have to keep up with what the public knows. It could be that I've been spotted somewhere, or Junior's been pinched en route to the Holtzes.

"Yes, Jim. You're trending on social media."

"Really? Trending, huh? What are they saying about me?"

"Here's a few samples."

Click.

Samantha's voice is replaced by a young woman's nasal voice: "Oh my god, have you seen this FBI-wanted psycho named Jim? I don't know what he's wanted for, but that *hair* is a crime against humanity!"

Click.

Another voice, male: "A courageous young man named Max Maddison blew the whistle on this twerp named Jim, owner of J & J—"

"That's enough, Samantha!"

"Yes, Jim."

"Fuck those social media parasites," I mutter.

I glance back at Doc, who's crouched in the rear of the meat wagon, separated from the front by a perforated sheet of metal. He's surrounded by medical paraphernalia we've picked up along the way. The wagon's shelves have never been fuller, with all sorts of crap Doc sticky-fingered from hospitals as we traveled south from Oak Falls to Carson City.

Doc and Samantha have been busy analyzing the cell-regenerating aloe medicine we used at Oak Falls High. We've got a big vat of it in the back, thanks to that stupid ponytailed girl and that pathetic worm Maxwell. Ha! When that silly bastard sees what I've created, he'll shit himself. Stupid nervous fuck—you take from me, and I take from you ten times!

Anyway, Doc and Samantha have even found a way to make the medicine stronger. I don't know how, and frankly, I don't give a shit. All I asked is that they make sure that it's ready for our upcoming operations and, most importantly, to keep our highest priority patient alive.

"How's our precious cargo doing back there, Howson?"

Doc jams his finger against her neck. "She's dehydrated, and this dry heat isn't helping." He rummages through the shelves. "I need rehydration solutions—we're out!"

"Well, Doc, we can't have her croaking on us, so I'd suggest you buy her some electrolytes or whatever the fuck you need to keep her alive."

"Yes, Jim."

"Do you have everything else you need for our upcoming event? We're expecting a full house, and you seem distracted."

"No, no, all systems are a go, Jim. We're all set."

"Bravo, Doc. Now get your legs in gear and hop to it. We have a long-ass ride ahead of us."

Doc exits the meat wagon and hustles toward the Walgreens. I turn my attention to the passenger seat beside me, where lies a red-haired mullet scalp that I sliced from my stupid-ass second cousin.

I slip the ginger scalp over my hair and adjust its position in the rearview mirror. I must say that I look ridiculous, but my gorgeous natural locks are a dead giveaway. I fire up the meat wagon's engine.

"Samantha, how do I look?"

"Jim, I'm afraid I can't see you."

"Not yet, baby, but real soon you will."

5. I DON'T HAVE ALL DAY

THE FINAL PIECE OF NEWS I CAUGHT BEFORE unplugging myself from the internet was a live national broadcast that covered the pre-trial hearing of Washington State's ex-Governor Louise Holtz and her husband. They were charged with mass murder, human trafficking, coercion, environmental crimes, crimes against humanity, racketeering, and corruption, all of which the SD card I'd swallowed corroborated with undeniable evidence.

"Max ..."

I watched it on my phone. Handcuffed and garbed in hideous fluorescent-orange jumpsuits, the Holtzes were marched up a flight of marble stairs to a courtroom where they faced a judge, who denied bail due to their flight risk and the enormity of their charges.

The local and national news stations flooded the world with stories about the Oak Falls Massacre. From Bellingham to Boston, 24-hour live coverage explained every grim detail of the entire operation. It was an historic moment; a Washington state governor had never been tossed out of office with steel around their wrists.

"Hey ..."

Soon, thousands of furious people were picketing and marching around the state capitol building in Olympia, screaming, "Lock 'em up!" and "Eat the rich!" They were overturning police vehicles and setting dumpsters on fire.

I watched all this go down from the safety of the St. Joseph Medical Hospital waiting room in Bellingham. As much as I wanted to join the public demonstration in Olympia against the Holtzes, I couldn't. After everything that happened, I just didn't have the energy.

"Max!"

The entire situation was horrific: the tainted coffee filters, the organ harvesting, the mind-controlled minions—all covered up with a fake disease by the governor. Lies upon lies upon lies. A bloody shit-stain in the history books.

"We're losing him ..."

The news hadn't let up by the time we left the hospital, and I was feverish from reliving the horrible events. I was watching the broadcasts on YouTube non-stop until I couldn't take it anymore.

"Yo! Dude! You with us, buddy?"

And now, *another* catastrophe ravaging our state? How often does lightning strike twice in the same spot?

"Max!" Carter snaps, and I shake away my hellish memories. "What are we going to do?"

There are two Carters and two Sunshines standing before me. The living room is spinning, and I think I'm about to hurl. But somehow, I muster the energy to spit out four words, four words that have been burning inside of me for weeks. I whimper, "I need a fix!"

Carter snatches his phone from my hand, shaking his head. "Wrong! Bad, Max!" Carter yells as if disciplining a dog.

"I do! I need a fix or else I'll—"

WHACK! Sunshine slaps me clean across my cheek.

I stagger from shock and fall to one knee. My face burns—a hot, stinging sensation runs up my jawline to my ear. "Ouch," I yelp. "What the hell?"

"Jesus, cuz. That was some slap," Carter whistles as he side-steps around me toward the sofa.

"Snap out of it, Max!" Sunshine points her finger at me sternly. "You promised us you'd stop! You said you'd focus on dealing with your problems instead of being dependent on those damn lights."

I suddenly remember the last time I tried to get a fix. I left her and Carter in a panic, got thrown in the slammer, and Sunshine wound up kidnapped with her house set on fire.

I get to my feet, and just as I'm about to tell her that she's right and that I'm sorry, Carter thrusts his palm at Sunshine. "Pay up," he says to his cousin. "That counts, and you know it. Come on, I don't have all day."

Sunshine lets out an exaggerated sigh, reaches into her pocket to pull out a ten-dollar bill, and drops it in Carter's hand.

"You need to learn how to breathe, Max," she says, taking a seat on the sofa next to her cousin.

"You want to go double or nothing?" Carter taunts her. The cousins erupt into a fit of laughter. For a straight minute, which feels like forever when you're the butt-end of a joke, their bellies pulsate as they laugh until they have tears running down their faces. I'm burning up, not from the slap but from humiliation.

I ask, "What's so funny, you two?" My question causes them to laugh even harder than before. Their chuckles grow an octave higher and louder, breaking the needle off an imaginary laugh-o-meter in my mind.

Carter sputters the words between gasps, "His

... face ... priceless!" He wipes his eyes and shakes his head. He can't keep a grip on his phone and it drops to his side.

"Oh, Carter, this was too cruel," Sunshine says, but she's grinning.

A second later, I get the joke. The article is a fake. They made a bet on how I would react.

"You bastards," I mumble, reaching for Carter's phone from the cushion between them. Carter snatches it up and clenches it with both hands, tight against his gut as if it were a pigskin fumble.

If only we were playing full-contact football—I would slam that shithead to the ground. "Give it here!" I bark.

The bald bastard giggles. "No way."

"Let me see it," I demand.

"You already did," he says, and the cousins burst into renewed laughter.

I'm pissed off. Still, I don't want to make an even bigger ass out of myself, so I back off. I park my butt on the La-Z-Boy's armrest and cross my arms. "Ha, ha. Real funny. You two sure fooled me."

"That look on your face ... fucking ... priceless," Carter repeats. He's still shaking, reminding me of the times we'd get buzzed off cheap hooch as teenagers.

Sunshine tries to steady herself. "I ... I'm so ... sorry ... Max ... it was Carter's idea."

"Hey, you helped," Carter says. "I can't believe you *slapped* him. That was way off-script. Oh God, my ribs hurt ... worth it!"

Sunshine says contritely, "Obviously it was too much, too soon. It won't happen again."

"Whatever," I say gruffly. "If you two will excuse me, I need some fresh air."

"Max, you'd be laughing too if you could have seen your face," Carter says.

"You're unbelievable, Carter, you know that? And for your information, that bogus article was sloppy, amateur work at best, and that slap was ... well, I've had worse." I jump to my feet.

"Come on, buddy, don't leave," Carter says. "Anyway, tell Crutch that, he did all the—"

That little ginger's in on it too? They're all ganging up on me like this?

"Well, har-de-fuckin'-har. I'm glad everyone is having a fun time at my expense." I snatch my half-eaten maple bar from the coffee table. "Thanks for breakfast, Sunshine. Tell Chuck I'll be back at eleven." I stomp toward the door, open it, and turn to say, "You two are something else. Have a *wonderful* day."

"Oh come on Max, don't be like—"
SLAM!

I take off down the street, running like a madman pumped up on PCP. I feel my blood coursing hot through my veins as I race around a roundabout.

I need a place to lie low for a while and cool my jets, but I don't want to go back to my apartment. Where, then?

My feet know the answer before I do. It's the least likely spot in the world you'd think a person with my history would run to, but I assure you I'm sane—clear-minded, level-headed, and perfectly lucid.

I run straight for J & J Funeral.

6. Spring of Deception

Noah was my body-hauling partner at J & J. When I spoke with the Feds after my friends and I blew the whistle on the Holtzes' vile operation, I let them know Noah was chipped, and thus innocent of any wrongdoing.

I kind of had to, because otherwise, we might have lost one of our own. Sunshine could also have been implicated in the Oak Falls Massacre. For crying out loud, she chopped up bodies, stuffed them into a meat grinder, and turned their guts into fertilizer—including my own mother. She'd been chipped too, and since she has zero memory of her heinous crimes, I figured that Noah too was innocent.

Thinking back, Noah was spot on about one thing; the crooked, mother-killing, Beast-stealing asshole we both once called Boss, Jim, *had* treated him like family. After the dust had settled, Noah became the director of J & J Funeral.

I read it in the papers. A notarized document surfaced, stating that if Jim was ever not mentally fit or alive or for any reason unable to act as funeral director, Noah would oversee all business decisions and operations at J & J Funeral. And since Jim was on the run from the FBI and clearly unable to perform his duties, Noah took them on.

After Noah was handed the keys to the funeral home, his initial order of business was to give back to the community. How? By gifting burial plots and gravestones to the victims' families.

Now, this might not sound like the most touching way to give back to a town that has suffered such huge losses, but don't forget that the cost of burying the dead is astronomical.

How much, you ask? The price depends on the burial plot's location, size, and its gravestone. Your run-of-the-mill gravestones start at around a thousand bucks, and each letter etched costs between $75 to $300, depending on font size and style. Luxurious gravestones, the ones you see from a hundred yards away made of Italian marble and etched with lengthy verses in ornate fonts, well, something like that could run north of a luxury car or a small home.

Over the years, as cemetery plots have become less available, the cost is no longer the issue; the problem is that you're forced to play the funeral lottery. I'm not kidding. People pay to throw their names in a hat in hopes to be lucky enough to own a piece of dirt.

You might think: Screw all that, I'll just dig my own doggone six-foot hole in my backyard. Well, I won't stop you, just don't get caught—it's a serious crime. Don't do it, even if you have a notarized statement from the deceased requesting, "Honey, dump my remains under the apple tree in our backyard." In Washington State, you'll get slapped with a minimum of three years in the slammer plus lawyer fees up the yin-yang. Even if you were, as you might say in court, "fulfilling my loved one's wishes for their remains, your honor."

In short, if you want your loved ones buried legally, you'll have to go to a business. And if you live in Whatcom County, that business is J & J Funeral, the largest cemetery in the state.

Since the massacre, the state has needed to deal with thousands of bodies. Cemeteries everywhere are slammed. "A serious fucking payday," as Jim might have put it. Noah, though, has been giving away plots for free.

Noah even made his way back to Oak Falls High and retrieved my mother personally. Well ... one part of her, at least. My mother's body had been chewed to unrecognizable bits and pink mush from an industrial meat grinder—all except her hand, which he transported back to J & J Funeral.

Noah had phoned to ask if I knew where my father was buried at J & J. "The records weren't computerized when he was buried," he explained. "And boy, are the paper files a mess. Anyway, your mother's plot is supposed to be next to his."

"What do you mean?" I asked him. I was nine when my father passed away, and I fainted in the middle of his funeral; I've never visited his grave since. So I didn't even remember that he was buried at J & J's cemetery, much less the exact location of his plot.

I explained this to Noah and he described the cemetery grounds in detail, hoping to jog my memory, but nothing rang a bell. The next week, Noah called back to tell me that he'd located my father's plot near the southern entrance, aisle F, row seventeen, and he would soon be burying my mother next to him.

I didn't make it to the burial. I was busy at Chuck's. The big guy needed my help, and besides, my mother's remains were nothing but a bucket of blood with her hand floating in it, so it wasn't like a *real* funeral. It's not like anybody else attended either—not her relatives, not even a pastor. Noah's too short-staffed to arrange individual rites for everyone. He's got hundreds of bodies to deal with, and he's gotta bury them fast before they start to stink—if the rats don't get to them first.

At least today, I can tell her goodbye.

I run out of breath about two miles from Chuck's place; cardio isn't my strongest suit. My phone's GPS tells me it'll be a while until I reach the southern entrance of J & J Funeral by walking. Plenty of time to think.

The sun wants to break through the clouds, and folks who are brand new to this corner of the world might think that it will be a beautiful day —*summer is right around the corner, so I better get my swimsuit out from the bottom of my closet.* As a native Washingtonian, I'll tell you that Mother Nature is lying.

I've heard that there's eleven seasons in Washington, and they go something like this: winter, then fool's spring, a second winter, then a spring of deception, a third winter with lots of rain, which becomes mud season before it's actually spring, first summer followed by a false fall, a second summer which lasts a week or two, then the actual fall. Today is the spring of deception, and soon, relentless rain will be on its way. Mother Nature likes practical jokes.

Jokes—I'm still ticked off by the cousins' shitty joke from earlier. I can usually take a joke. It's far from the first prank Carter has ever played on me, and I normally shake off the humiliation after a few minutes. But this one, *this* joke, has me beating myself up.

As I replay my actions in my head, I realize that I kind of lost it back there. Practical jokes are the cornerstone of my relationship with Carter; we've been messing with each other since we were kids. Looking back at how I reacted, I feel like an utter fool.

I lost my cool, but why? What was the real reason behind my overblown reaction, slamming the door and leaving all hot and bothered like a child throwing a tantrum at recess?

Wait! I get it. It's so obvious now—I freaked out because Sunshine was in on Carter's shenanigans this time, and that confirmed what I've been dreading ... no! ... It's clear to me now how she thinks about me. Crap, I'm in the *friend* zone.

Everyone knows once you've entered the *friend* zone, there's no turning back. You're stuck as friends forever, and that's what's gnawing at me. There's no chance in hell that we'll be anything else.

I'm close now—I can make out the J & J entrance up ahead. The sun has broken through, and there's even a rainbow arcing above. I know too well this fair weather is temporary, and I try to push away my thoughts and focus on the beauty of this moment.

Still, a dark voice repeats in my head that it doesn't change the fact that I'm in the *friend* zone.

7. The clock is ticking

Samantha tells me to take the NV-265 to the US-95 South, avoiding the route through California so we don't cross any more state lines; she's such a brilliant bitch. This route puts us straight through Las Vegas. As much as I'd love to hit the Strip and roll some dice, Doc reminds me that our patient is fragile, and time is of the essence.

We shove on, hauling ass down the US-93 to the AZ-303 on the outskirts of Phoenix. A quick skip to the US-10, then southbound on the AZ-85 until we exit onto the main drag of Snake Bend, then we hang a left onto Gospel Way. Further down, a right through a double iron gate takes us onto a semi-circular driveway.

Samantha has guided us safely on our sixteen-hundred-mile journey from Oak Falls to Snake Bend, a small desert town some eighty miles north of the Mexican border. It's the perfect place for the next phase of Project Exodus, as it's quiet and sparsely populated. That suits me just fine, because what I don't need is another bunch of local snooping assholes.

As I slow down, Samantha intones with robotic finality, "You have arrived at the Church of the Holy Desert."

My eyes feast upon the grandest structure I have ever seen. Samantha continues as if addressing tourists cruising the streets on a double-fucking-decker, "Sixty thousand square feet of meticulously crafted stone, marble, iron, and wood, designed by architect Thomas Thornwood, who used the Roman Colosseum as inspiration. Its shape is cylindrical, with wrap-around doorways and dozens of arched windows."

"Thanks for the architecture lesson," I tell her.

Honey, I'm fucking home, and for now this is all mine. Holy smokes, it's more glorious than I ever imagined it would be. I tilt my head upward to admire its towering dome, bathed in the afternoon light. Rising from its center are two steeples with sharp points that tear into the sky, piercing a fluffy cloud above like it's a marshmallow on a roasting fork.

Taking in this sublime megachurch gets me all misty-eyed. I tremble from the overwhelming aura of this holy structure. I feel as if God Himself is looking down at yours truly, approving of my presence. The stars have blessed me and provided safe passage, leading me to my newfound sanctuary, making it clear beyond all doubt that I am the chosen one, come to save souls lost in excess, lost in the evils of the world. And I tell you, this day marks the beginning of a new chapter that will go down in the history books. Yes! A newborn way of living in harmony that I, Jim, shall safeguard for as long as I shall live!

I maneuver my meat wagon toward the front door. But to call it a simple door would be a terrible understatement, for this *threshold* must be over sixteen feet tall. Constructed from solid mahogany and iron hardware, it—like everything else in this church—must have cost a small fortune. I kill the engine, rip the ginger mullet scalp from my head, and let out a sigh of relief.

Samantha asks, "Are you alright, Jim?"

"I'm A-OK," I tell her. She no longer needs electricity from the meat wagon to sustain herself. She's getting stronger on her own, thanks to Doc's excellent engineering in updating her systems, and after tonight, she won't need the meat wagon whatsoever.

"It's game time, Doc," I say, adjusting the rearview mirror to look at him. "You know the plan. First, take care of Samantha, then the essentials, and there's a shit-ton of people headed here as we speak, all wanting to be saved. Are you ready for the big push?"

Doc runs his nervous old-man hands through the white hairs of his head, making some of them stand straight up like he's been electrocuted. "Yes, Jim. Ready as I'll ever be, but ... well, do you happen to know when Junior and the Holtzes are supposed to arrive?"

"For the third time, Doc, Junior will be here with the Holtzes early tomorrow morning. Got it? Now come on, Howson, I need your head in the game." I twist in my seat, no longer looking at Doc via his reflection. "Get moving, and take good care of Samantha, got me?"

Doc sighs, slumping as he exhales deeply. "I got it, Jim, but—"

"No buts about it, Doc! Now I recognize that you're overwhelmed, maybe even scared a little. Hell, I might be too if I were in your shoes. But we've been working together for a long time now, Doc, and I know what you're capable of. I believe in you!"

"But, still ... Jim, I don't know if—"

"Doctor Howson! I'll have none of that weakness. Don't you forget for one second that you're an extraordinary doctor, and you're going to help us achieve greatness. And it starts with a new empowered attitude, so chin up and walk the block like you got a pair!"

Doc sits up straight. "Yes, Jim. Greatness."

"You're damn fucking right, Doc. Walk tall and proud because this is our kingdom now, and together, we'll achieve the unthinkable! Now, clear out the meat wagon, starting with our prized specimen. The clock is ticking."

8. Subdued Excitement

My father's gravestone is weathered and crooked like a backwoods bastard's bucktooth in sore need of a dentist's tender care. It protrudes from an overgrown snarl of long grasses and clovers. It's engraved with the name MADDISON—just like the one next to it.

The sod at my mother's plot is freshly turned; nothing yet grows there. Her last recognizable remnants are decomposing beneath me. Six feet under, just like she promised.

I drop to my knees between my parents' graves, trembling. *I'm an orphan.* They're gone, and I'm alone in the world. Blood rushes into my skull and rises to the surface of my skin. I'm heating up. Everything aches all of a sudden.

Exhaling slowly, I collapse backward onto the

soft grassy ground. Flailing my hands, I tear out fistfuls of the grass around me and beat the earth with my fists. My mouth opens, and words start flying out beyond my control. "I'm sorry! I'm so sorry! I wish I was stronger! Smarter! I'm so fucking sorry!"

I yell until I lose my voice and the strength to continue, then I lie there, limp and spent. Breathing in, I smell the intense green scent of the torn grass around me. Rays of sunshine warm my skin like a comforting blanket. They remind me of my therapy lights, and of something—*someone*—else I don't want to think about. I shut my eyes and instantly, I'm out like a light.

When I awaken, I'm shivering and disoriented. The sun has set below the horizon, and in its place, a waxing moon hovers above my head. I slept through the whole day. Holy shit, I'm alone at night in a graveyard.

I spring to my feet, brushing off blades of grass. I feel a tap on my shoulder from behind, and I spin around to behold a dark figure, gripping what looks like a scythe in one hand and a dim lantern in the other. Its face is shadowed by a deep hood, and it's completely silent. Did I die in my sleep? Is this the Grim Reaper here to take my soul away?

Terrified, I back away until my heel hits my

mother's gravestone, causing me to stumble and fall. The figure lowers the lantern, brings it closer to its face, and says, "Max, you're awake."

"Noah?"

He tosses his hoodie back from his head. "Yeah, it's me."

"Jesus. You scared the living crap out of me."

"Are you okay?" Noah offers me his hand, but I wave it off.

"I'm peachy. Must have dozed off is all." I haul myself up.

"Sorry if I startled you." Noah smiles, exposing his oversized Tom Petty teeth. The sight is reassuring; it somehow solidifies that he is, in fact, Noah, and not some soul-snatching underworld demon.

"You've been sleeping here for a while," he says, looking me over. I catch his eyes pause at my dirt-streaked fists, and I shove my hands into the ass pockets of my jeans. "I noticed you earlier, must have been around noon. I didn't disturb you because you were either dead—in which case, take a number!—or you really needed your sleep. I circled back after finishing up a few burials and saw that you were still here." Noah gestures with his lantern behind me and says, "Like it? I had her gravestone rush ordered."

"Thanks, Noah. It's perfect." I'm touched. My

attention swings to the shovel in Noah's hand. Its sharp tip glints in the lantern light. In my earlier terror, I'd thought it was a scythe. "Have you been hand-digging graves?"

"Have to—by any means necessary. You know what I mean," he says, and I think back on the time we dragged a 400-pound stiff out of a building through a window, using my Beast and a strap tied around the corpse's swollen ankles. Yep, I knew what he meant.

"The John Deere's clutch pack needs replacing," Noah says. "So I'm doing it old school for now. The ground's been warming up, so it's getting easier to dig. It's honest exercise, you know, but there's just so many of them. Luckily I managed to grab the refrigerators from Oak Falls High."

He sounds tired, and I take a closer look at him. Noah looks different without his hazmat suit. He's replaced the old silver-condom getup with street clothes—black hoodie, denim work jeans, boots—but what's most startling to me is his face. He's unshaven, with enormous bags under his eyes, and looks like he's aged a decade within a few weeks.

Noah continues, "Max, I've been meaning to tell you something for a while now."

"Tell me what?"

"I owe you one."

"Cut the crap, Noah. We already talked about this. You don't owe me a thing."

"Yes, I do!" he cries, dropping his shovel to the ground. "I wouldn't be here if it wasn't for you and what you told the FBI. My ass would be in prison."

"Noah, don't worry about it. All I did was tell the truth. Jim chipped you and controlled your mind. What else was there for me to tell them?"

"Still, you didn't have to, and I'm not so sure I would have done the same thing in your shoes if it was me who helped kill your mother."

That one stings. Yes, he's technically correct, but him being chipped trumps his argument. If I blamed him, I'd have to blame Sunshine too.

"Noah, again, you don't owe me anything. Okay? Let's forget the past for a second. Look at how much you've been helping our community—with or without a working tractor."

Noah relaxes and shoves his free hand into his jeans pocket, searching within its depths. "Well," he says, "maybe this will make us even." He pulls out something shiny. "I couldn't bury it with her. I thought you might want it."

I recognize it as soon as I see it.

"Take it," Noah says. "Just don't tell anyone where you got it."

I take my mother's wedding ring from his grasp and stare at it in the moonlight. All my life, I had never seen it off her ring finger, not once. "Noah, I—I don't know what to say except ... thank you."

"It was nothing."

"This is more than nothing, Noah. We're square." I shove the ring into my jeans' fifth pocket.

"Thanks for saying that, Max." Noah's eyes light up. "Hey! Did you hear that the judge denied the Holtzes' bail?"

"Yeah, and if you ask me, those bastards deserve a hundred life sentences for what they did."

"I still can't believe it happened here. In Bellingham, of all places."

"What happened to the City of Subdued Excitement, right?"

Noah nods. "I think Bellingham should have a new city slogan."

"Oh?"

"I've been thinking about it, and I don't think the old one describes us anymore. It should be the City of Graves, or how about Home of the Oak Falls Massacre? ..." Noah trails off when he notices me casting a glance at my parents' plots. "Sorry, Max. It's a stupid joke."

"No, it's funny, I like it. Hell, make some shirts and sell them at the Farmers Market."

My phone vibrates, alerting me that I have unread text messages.

Carter: *Dude, where did you go?*

Sunshine: *Sorry again, Max. I'll see you tomorrow.*

Crutch: *Coming?*

Shit! I'm late for my shift. I text Crutch back to let him know that I'm on my way. "Noah, I've got to—"

Noah scratches the back of his neck in an all-too-familiar way. I'm hit by a flashback: Crutch's older brother Quinn slashing that silicon out of his neck, and Noah's blood spurting everywhere. My hackles rise. I stop talking and take a few steps back, my hands lifting to a defensive position.

Noah yanks his hand away from his neck. "Sorry," he says. "The scar still itches sometimes."

I lower my guard. "I bet," I tell him. "Hey, I've got to run. Thanks for everything. I'll catch up with you later, okay?" As the words leave my mouth, I'm struck by a strange certainty that I will never see Noah again.

"Sure, see you around, Max." Noah scratches at his neck once more.

"Oh, and Noah—I got it."

"Got what, Max?"

"A new town slogan."

He tilts his head as if to say, out with it.

"Chip City," I say with a smile.

Noah's eyebrows rise and his lips begin to quaver with mirth. I turn and take off down the grassy hill, sprinting toward the southern gate.

My phone buzzes. It's another message, but I don't bother with it because I'm already a long way from Chuck's place, and if there's one thing the big guy hates, it's tardiness.

9. Short of Extraordinary

Fun fact: megachurches are equipped with advanced medical equipment. Why? Preachers can't afford people falling to the floor mid-sermon from a heart attack or stroke and dying before thousands of their peers because there's no defibrillator in the House of God.

As you may already know, I'm an expert in the body removal business, and sudden death during a religious service happens more often than you might think. There are at least forty-five church-goers a month in the U.S. who end up croaking mid-sermon.

Don't believe me? What do you say we calculate some arithmetic together?

The average age of a churchgoer in America is fifty-six, and we all know that once you hit fifty-four, your chances of experiencing a fatal cardiac explosion or stroke double. Over five hundred thousand souls leave the earth this way every year. How many keel over in a church? Significant numbers, considering the U.S. is home to the most megachurches in the world, and each of their megastructures have the capacity for ten-thousand-plus Bible-thumpers to pray together under one roof. Not to mention that the average megachurch service lasts seven-and-a-half hours.

When such a tragic event takes place and a church is revealed to lack proper medical equipment, meaning Grandpa Johnny died when his death could have been prevented, the congregation starts asking questions. Questions like, "How can our church's leaders have such disregard for their flock?" Their concerns spew over into social media—"House of God becomes a pit of death!" Online memes spread like a virus, triggering a wave of lawsuits and ultimately bankrupting the church in question.

Not great for business. So here, the Church of the Holy Desert was built with a medical facility that fucking Johns Hopkins Hospital itself would drool over. Underneath the megachurch's auditorium lies a state-of-the-art medical facility that can support up to twenty-plus patients at a time. This holy hospital includes smooth, self-sanitizing surfaces, high-tech diagnostic and imaging equipment, advanced monitoring systems, ventilators, and of course, defibrillators. The operating rooms are equipped with high-tech tools that would give any surgeon a wet dream.

I asked Doc what his thoughts were about the medical facility. His eyes were cloudy, and I believe a tear fell down his cheek when he said, "Remarkable, Jim. I've never seen anything quite like it in all my years of medicine."

Earlier, Doc popped the hood of the meat wagon and detached Samantha's CPU from the vehicle's electronics. Then he emptied the back of our supplies, including our sole remaining vat of aloe medicine, and gurneyed our precious patient to the surgery room. The doors closed, and Doc went to work for several hours. I've been waiting, as impatient as a soon-to-be father in a maternity ward.

Finally, Doc pages me through our wireless headsets. "Jim, come down here. It's done!"

I'm in the dressing room, combing my hair and trying to find the perfect outfit for the kickoff, but I stop what I'm doing and hustle to the church's basement. When the chrome doors of the elevator slide open, I see Doc in the hallway—covered in blood.

I cry out, "Is *she* okay?"

It's then that our patient emerges from the operating room. She turns toward me with a smile and says, "Hello, I'm Samantha. You must be Jim. It's so nice to finally see you."

My God. I never believed it could work. I squeeze Doc's shoulder. "You sonofabitch, you did it! You brilliant fucking man—I can't believe what I'm seeing."

"Thank you, Jim," Doc says. "I have a few more tests to run, but yes, I believe the operation was a great success."

I examine Samantha closely. Her eyes are light hazel with dark lashes that match her messy shoulder-length hair. She's clothed in a thin paper medical gown, and her skin glistens with a thin coating of the aloe medicine.

I run the back of my hand against Samantha's cheek, across her chin, then along the back of her neck, where my fingers brush against electrical wires. They're rolled and zip-tied into a rope, with one end plugged into the back of her head and the other tied into a small box, her main processing unit.

I advance my hand down her slick arm, passing her elbow, and stop once I reach her wrist. I apply pressure with my fingertips. She has a faint pulse, yet she's cool to the touch. I release my grip and gaze upon my new obsession, my love, my Samantha—she's perfect.

"Will she be ready to shoot our promo soon?" I ask Doc.

"Well, given the extent of the operation, it's crucial to allow adequate time for her neural tissues to properly heal. She's been uploaded with over three petabytes of data, and her brain needs to stabilize. The inflammation must resolve to avoid complications, and engaging in premature activities could delay her recovery time signifi—"

"For fuck's sake, Doc, how much time will she need?"

"Yes, umm, a day at least. But maybe sooner with the aloe. She'll need a constant coating of it."

While Doc and I are having our little exchange, Samantha does not move so much as an inch. Nor did she flinch when I caressed her face. She just stands there silently, though her eyes track my every move.

"Doc, are you sure she's okay?"

"Oh yes, very much so. Like I mentioned, she'll need time, but I assure you that her brain is healing diligently even as we speak."

I lean into her and whisper, "Samantha, what is your purpose?"

She blinks twice, then turns her chin up toward me. "Jim, my purpose is to serve you."

I whisper, "And how will you serve me?"

"Jim, let me remind you that I have already been serving. While bound to the meat wagon, I searched the medical records of millions of Americans, targeting compatible blood types and specimens of appropriate age. With that data, I contacted them through the internet, creating ads based on their interests. Through these online ads, many signed up to join Project Exodus. At this moment, those essentials are traveling here, seeking to bask in your greatness, seeking change, seeking a way out of their miserable lives. And we'll show them that way, thanks to the new microchips I designed with Doc. And now that I am no longer merely a machine but fully embodied, I will continue to serve you, no matter the obstacles."

Her words send chills down my spine. I'm so choked with bliss that I can't swallow, and as my heart thumps, I mutter, "Fan-fuckin'-tastic work, Howson."

"And Jim," Doc says, "just wait until she's one hundred percent recovered. There's much more than meets the eye. I assure you, Samantha will be nothing short of extraordinary."

10. Small and Silly

By the time I reach Chuck's driveway, my legs are burning, and I'm breathing like I've got half a lung. I leap over Crutch's red Schwinn and burst through the door. The moment I'm inside, my eardrums are pulverized by high-energy '80s techno.

Crutch sits on a chair pulled close to the Zenith TV in the living room, his torso twitching back and forth. To his right is Chuck, wearing a burgundy bathrobe and seated on his throne, the La-Z-Boy.

They're oblivious to my presence, and as I approach them, I realize what has them so entranced. They're playing a video game—Contra for NES, I think—but they're mashing buttons on what look like wireless PlayStation controllers.

I take a seat on the sofa-slash-my-bed behind

them and watch, unnoticed. The Zenith's screen pulsates with seizure-inducing flashes. Bombs explode as bullets destroy robotic alien enemies. The game's techno soundtrack sounds like the original Contra, but it's not—it's been sped up. Is this a turbo mod? The characters are different, too. There's a werewolf creature with a bazooka slung over its furry shoulder, and a cute bot that looks like a steel thimble.

The characters run, spin, and shoot their way through a post-apocalyptic setting. In the game, an evil-looking machine with six mechanical arms and one large eye bursts from the ground. "Die, sucker!" Chuck hollers. The werewolf somersaults into the air, evading the enemy machine in the nick of time, and fires his bazooka —BOOM!

A strobe of orange and crimson fireballs consumes the screen like a detonated nuke. Injured, the six-armed machine burrows back down to where it came from, and the game's music speeds up and amplifies. The screen strobes as the machine emerges again in a different spot.

"Jump over here!" Crutch yells over the deafening sound effects. His bot climbs the side of a brick wall—a classic Contra move—and the werewolf follows, gripping the wall with his claws.

"Get some!" Crutch shouts, and a purple laser shoots out from his bot's eyes, destroying the arms and torso of the evil machine and reducing it to its head.

The eye in the head blinks—it's not over.

"Wait ... for ... it," Chuck says, anticipating the next move.

The screen lights up as a laser beam unleashes from the eye, spinning clockwise. The werewolf leaps into the air, avoiding the laser, but the bot isn't so lucky—it collides with the death beam and disintegrates into oblivion.

"Balls!" Crutch swears. The kid drops his now-useless controller to the carpet. Turning to Chuck, he coaches, "Use your specialty weapon!"

"Copy that!" Chuck hammers a complex combination of buttons. The werewolf raises his bazooka above his head. "Sayonara, suckers!" Chuck yells, and the screen erupts in a cataclysm. The enemy machine's head topples over onto the smoldering rubble and explodes. The music fades, the words STAGE CLEAR appear, then the credits roll. Chuck and Crutch scream in unison, "WOOO-HOOOOO!"

"We destroyed that evil bastard!" Crutch shouts as they high-five each other. Above the rolling credits is the title: CONTRA HARD CORPS. Never heard of it.

Crutch helps Chuck out of his chair, and they dance around the living room in a broken waltz. Chuck's ankle must be feeling better. They stop once they notice me in the room and back away from each other, their faces turning cherry-red.

I slow clap as I say, "Bravo! Well done, you two. You saved the world."

Crutch takes a knee with his arms out and theatrically says, in a botched British accent, "Thank you, sir, but it's *he* who has defeated our enemy." He points to Chuck, who takes a bow before settling back into his seat.

"Holy cow, that game is nothing but eight-bit adrenaline!" Chuck exclaims. "Almost as intense as being caught in enemy crossfire—ha! Balls-to-the-walls fun, that's what it is."

Crutch reaches behind the Zenith and pulls out some sort of dongle, causing the screen to dissolve into static. He gathers the controllers from the floor and shoves them and the dongle into his olive-green JanSport backpack. Reaching behind the TV once more, he fiddles until the static on the tube becomes live local news.

"—friction abroad has prompted the U.S. President to schedule a mandatory meeting with officials later today as tension rises in the East—"

Click. Crutch twists the power knob and the TV screen turns dark. He hoists his backpack onto his shoulders, adjusts the straps, and says, "Well, that was fun, sir."

"Sir? Crutch, we just saved the world together. You better call me Chuck."

Crutch nods. "Okay, Chuck." He extends his pale, freckled hand toward the big guy for a shake.

"Darn tootin'!" Chuck says, then does something I've never seen him do before. He and Crutch exchange three sideways hand slaps, bap-bap-bap. This is followed by a fist bump, an elbow tap, then a series of complex smacks, waves, and wiggles I couldn't even begin to describe.

What the hell? I've never had a secret handshake with Chuck.

Crutch approaches me and says, "Sorry about that news article, Max. Carter asked me to put it together, but I didn't know the joke was gonna be on you."

"It's cool, Crutch. I'll live," I tell him. I can't blame the kid. Carter must have pressured him somehow, just like he pressured me to drive to the Anderson Paper Mill that one fateful night.

The fact is, Crutch has been a tremendous help around here. He's been showing up every day, putting in his time without complaining or ever asking for anything. Sometimes I wonder what he gets out of it—then I remember that the little carrot top doesn't have anyone else in the entire world since the Oak Falls Massacre. He and I are a lot alike in that way.

Chuck kicks up the La-Z-Boy's foot rest and drawls, "Nasty trick to pull on someone, if you ask me. Reminds me of this time when I was stationed in West Texas. There was this guy, McFadden—knee-slapping funny guy with a thick Southern accent—anyway, he stole some military letterhead and typed up an elaborate letter stating that his bunkmate, Dunbar, was gonna get promoted and shipped out at 0700 hours to Camp Pendleton. Well, we watched Dunbar pack his bag, and before he took off, he gave our Sergeant a piece of his mind. But it didn't turn out so well, seeing as how there was no promotion, and Dunbar ended up doing pushups and laps for the next two weeks until he ..." Chucks trails off and frowns. "Well, shoot, come to think of it, it didn't end so well for ol' Dunbar. Sorry, Max—it sounded funnier in my head."

Great. Even Chuck has heard all about this practical joke, and they've probably heard how I stormed out like a baby, too. I feel the pity coming at me from all angles, and as a defense mechanism, I tell them, "Don't worry about it. It's nothing. I'm good." I plop down on the sofa. But that's a lie; I still feel small and silly.

Crutch tells us, "I'll see you guys tomorrow."

"Sounds good, Crutch, and sorry for not letting you know I was running late."

Crutch eyeballs my grass-stained pants and sleeves. "I'm sure you had a good reason." The kid waves and walks out the door.

"Max," Chuck says, "where did you go? You

look like you've been through hell and back. Don't tell me it was all because of my son's stupid, screwy prank."

"I'm fine. I was, err ... taking a nap in the grass is all." There's no reason to keep anything from Chuck; my whole life, he's been nothing but good to me. But I'm not in the right mindset to talk about where I've been, or about my life right now. Nothing personal.

"You were what?" Chuck leans toward me. "Napping? No, I know there's more to it than that. Carter!"

No response. Chuck shouts, "Carter Jackson, get your butt over here!"

Carter's voice reaches us from down the hallway. "What do you want now, Pops?"

"What I want, son, is for you to stop screwing with your buddy!"

"Wait, is Max here?" Carter trots into the living room.

"Chuck, it's okay," I say.

"Nonsense!" Chuck points at me while keeping his eyeballs on Carter. "Son, Max is helping us out. He and Sunshine and Crutch have been feeding us, picking up after us, making sure we're sleeping well through the night ... Am I right?" Chuck gets up from his La-Z-Boy, propping himself up with a hand on the backrest.

"Yeah, you're right," Carter says reluctantly.

"I know I am. And I'll say it again, don't screw with Max. *Comprende*?"

"It's not a problem," I mumble, embarrassed. "It was just a joke."

"Joke, Max?" Chuck turns to me sternly. "Don't downplay the situation at hand. My son needs to learn a valuable lesson." He turns back to Carter. "Now apologize to your best friend for messing with his head like that."

"Sorry," Carter says under his breath.

"What was that, son? We can't hear you."

"Sorry, Max. It was stupid, and it won't happen again."

"I shouldn't have been so sensitive," I say with a shrug.

"Sensitive, my ass!" Chuck yells. "Max, you've been dealing with a lot of crap, and you don't deserve any of it, particularly here. This place is as much your home as it is ours."

I nod, acknowledging his kind words.

"Great," Chuck says and sticks out his hand. "Now, put it here."

I roll myself off the sofa and extend my hand toward Chuck's. His enormous mitt swallows mine whole like a starving python consuming a field mouse. We shake, and I thank him.

He pats my shoulder, then turns to Carter. "Now, it's been a long day. Time for bed, don't you think, son?"

"I'll go to bed when I feel like it," Carter snaps. He stomps away and slams his bedroom door shut, and a few seconds later, heavy-metal music erupts from his bedroom.

"Good grief, what am I going to do with that one?" Chuck sighs. "That boy needs to learn when to put the kibosh on things before they get out of hand. Do you know what I'm saying, Max?"

I nod. I haven't got the nerve to explain to him the real reason that joke pissed me off. How Sunshine was in on it, and how that hurt the most. I mean, I can't talk to him about being in the friend zone with his *niece*.

Chuck winces and hunches over.

"Hey, are you okay?"

He waves my question off with both hands and flops onto the sofa. "Everything is great," he moans.

"Chuck, you said you were getting better."

"It is. ... I'm fine." He's not. He's sweating and gripping his gut.

"Let me see your stomach," I demand, scuttling closer to him.

Even though Chuck will always be *the big guy* to me, I can't help but notice that he's lost a lot of weight. I suspect that if he hadn't left the hospital after his liver transplant early, against medical advice—something about how sick bays remind him of 'Nam—he'd be better off today.

"No," Chuck protests. "It's nothing to sneeze at, but nothing I haven't dealt with before. Heck, after 'Nam, I had this nasty jungle boot rot between my toes. Now that is something worth going to the ER for, let me tell you. Boy, that fungus eats at your skin as if it's starving, kept me up for six months until my ex-wife told me to soak my toes in baking soda and lemon juice. I'm fine, Max. All good—"

I tug apart his bathrobe. Above his boxer shorts, his bandages are crusted with dried blood or pus or ... sickening thoughts race through my mind—a contagious disease, flesh-eating bacteria, death!

I snap out of it. "Oh geez," I groan. "Hold still, let me see what's going on here."

I begin to unravel the filthy dressings, but he swats my hands away, telling me, "Stop it, Max. It's just doing its thing—healing."

"Chuck, listen to me, I have to check under these bandages. I'm serious. Please."

He huffs and says, "Make it quick," then bites his lower lip.

I begin to pull apart the layers of gauze, but the pieces have fused into one. As I keep tugging, crusty scabs come off along with the dressing. Blood dribbles down his stomach.

"Jesus, Max, will you get on with it already? Yank it fast, like a Band-Aid."

"Whatever you say."

With one quick tug, I rip off the wrap, and it's worse than I imagined. The skin around the stitches is badly swollen and dripping with yellow pus. And fuck me, does it smell rancid, like Chinese takeout left out on the counter over a hot summer night.

"Chuck, I've got to take you to the hospital, like right now. That looks infected."

"Forget it, Max, it's not that bad. It'll heal up." Chuck glances down at the incision. "I think."

"Come on, let me clean you up at least."

"No. I'll take care of it."

"I'm serious. Grab my hand."

He reluctantly takes my hand, and I help him down the hall and into his bedroom. He releases a sharp breath with each step. We shuffle into the master bath.

Chuck takes a seat on the toilet lid while I plug the tub and let the water run. I grab his orange plastic bottle of anti-infection pills from the cabinet above the double his-and-hers sinks. I shake it—hardly a rattle. Last time I checked, it was almost full.

"What happened to all of your pills? Where are the rest of them?" I ask.

"They're gone. I flushed them."

"What? Why would you do a thing like that?"

"Well, for starters, they were making me itch

like crazy. Not to mention, giving me the runs all night."

"Chuck, these are for infection. You need them." Damn thick-headed Boomers, they think they can out-tough science. I massage my scalp with my fingertips. "Get in," I tell him, gesturing at the bathtub. "Once your stitches are clean, we're going straight to St. Joseph."

"No way, Max," he says, shaking his head. "I'll wash up, but I'm not going back there."

"Why not?"

"If they decide to keep me there, I won't survive another night lying on top of those crappy beds, listening to more of those damn machines beeping day and night."

I throw my hands up. "You're concerned about a bed? Beeps? Chuck, your gut looks like one of those rotting corpses from the Oak Falls High pit! Maybe I can't drag you to the hospital, but I'm calling Sunshine right now. When she sees this, she's going to be furious, and I don't blame her for a second. This is serious!"

"Geez Louise, Max, relax," Chuck says. "You sound like my ex-wife. I hear you, okay? Tell you what, if it makes you feel any better, I'll take a pill now and we can go to the hospital in the morning. Just let me get one more good night of sleep in my own bed, okay?"

"First thing tomorrow?"

"Yes. Scout's honor."

The bathtub's full, and I reach over to turn off the faucet. "Great. As soon as Sunshine gets here with your Jeep, we're going. I'll be back with the first-aid kit."

The big guy nods. As I walk out, he says my name and I turn.

"Yeah, Chuck?"

"Thanks, partner."

11. Free from pain

I don't want to come off like I'm ungrateful. With thousands of cushioned seats and a wrap-around balcony, the Church of the Holy Desert's auditorium is spectacular. It's equipped with a stereo system that would impress Sammy Hagar himself. However, the stage lacked a serious wow factor. It was bare, aside from a modest podium and microphone.

So I scoured the grounds for a prop, something both useful and beautiful, and soon stumbled upon what I needed: a cherrywood altar. Buried downstairs inside the church's baptismal chamber, it was a gorgeously carved chunk of wood that must weigh as much as a VW Bug. I explained to Samantha that I need this showpiece on stage. I don't know how she did it, but when I returned, she had it positioned front and center.

Samantha's not just strong and capable—she's a beauty, too. I have to admit, she looked a little rough around the edges right after her operation. She needed a makeover to be camera ready. Luckily, I found a dressing room with a closet full of fine female fashions, along with a vanity with a shit-ton of beauty products. I'm a man of many talents, and believe it or not, makeup artistry just so happens to be one of them. I earned top marks in Restorative Cosmetology at mortuary school.

As I prepared Samantha, Doc rigged up the church's slick media room to shoot our promo video. After the shoot, I set up a check-in system. Doc has already microchipped the first dozen essentials who trickled in, and I've put them straight to work as aides. They're such obedient little bastards. The aides escort incoming essentials from the parking lot and lead them into the grand auditorium.

Presiding behind the cherrywood altar onstage, I welcome our new arrivals into my circle of trust. As each approaches, I ask them to hand over their identification. I read their info out loud to Samantha because, for whatever reason, she can't read well. "Randy Star, male, thirty-three years of age, five-foot-seven, organ donor," I tell her.

Samantha cross-checks them in our database

by scanning their face with her eyes. "Randy Star, confirmed," she tells me.

Next, I have them sign a waiver, then ask for their keys, wallet, and any other valuables they might have, and toss it all into a security deposit box. Where we're going, they won't need 'em. Then, an aide ushers the newbie down the elevator to the operating room, where Doc prepares them for their promised transformation.

Doc's aides secure the essential face down on an operating table. They cinch the essential's wrists and ankles with leather straps and gag their mouth with a ball. We can't have them squirming or screaming while under the knife, and we don't have any anesthesia, so I can imagine that this is nothing short of absurdly painful.

Doc tells them to focus their attention on an inspirational painting of the Virgin Mary hung on the opposite wall. Then he fires up a handheld drill, the half-inch butterfly bit boring deep into the skull just above the vertebrae—but not so far as to disturb the sensitive cerebellum.

Next, Doc dips one of our newly designed silicon chips, shipped fresh from our overseas factory, into the vat of aloe medicine. He slides the aloe-coated chip deep into the essential's exposed brain, then seals their skull with a rubber plug and stitches up the gash, finishing with a dab of aloe. Soon, the essential is ready for orders, and their first task is to find their way back to the auditorium to join the rest of the reborn flock.

Now, to be clear, we're not doing anything illegal here. Not at all. Every person who shows up at our door is here by choice; nobody is kidnapping anyone, or killing them for that matter. What we're doing here is the exact opposite. We're giving them life! We're setting them free from pain, suffering, worry, and hunger, freeing them from their insignificant lives and empowering them to serve the greater good—yours truly!

12. Ninety-nine, One Hundred

The spring of deception has given way to the third winter. Hefty raindrops drum against the living room window as I toss and turn, struggling to sleep. But it's not Mother Nature who's to blame for my restlessness—it's Chuck. I can't erase the image of his hideous infection from my mind.

Cleaning up the big guy seemed to take hours. The swollen skin around his stitches burst, creating a geyser of pus and blood, turning the bath water into a shade of strawberry Kool-Aid. He was panicking; I'd never seen him so distressed, and I have to admit, I was on the verge of passing out myself.

It took two bath towels, a roll of gauze, and a healthy wad of duct tape before the hemorrhaging coagulated. It was well after one in the morning when I helped Chuck to his bed.

But my time as Nurse Max wasn't over. Chuck kept me up most of the night. He was moaning like a sick dog and needing to take a whiz every hour on the hour, and since he could hardly stand on his own two feet, I had to help him. I finally had enough and made him swallow four 800 milligrams of extra-strength Advil and another of his anti-infection meds. I haven't heard a peep out of him since.

I'm not upset about the work. I mean, this is what I signed up for. But what ticks me off is that his gut wouldn't have festered like that if Chuck hadn't flushed away his medication.

Fucking Boomers. The entire male half of his generation has been conditioned to never show weakness or ask for help, because help is for pansies—bite down and grind through it, soldier! Be the toughest guy in the room, no matter what's at stake! Thanks to this mentality, millions suffer in silence.

I love the big guy, I do, but what the fuck was he thinking? Infections like that don't just go away on their own. He's going to need some serious medical attention, maybe even more surgery to remove necrotic tissue, who knows?

Well, no sense in dwelling on what I can't change. What's done is done, and once Sunshine arrives, we'll rush him over to the emergency room, then I'll get some sleep. Now, where's my phone?

I find it wedged between two sofa cushions, and on its screen is a YouTube notification. Yeah, I know I claimed I deleted all my news apps. Well, I lied. Sorry, I could never delete my YouTube. At least I haven't been using it for news, only entertainment.

The notification is marked urgent, with hyperlinked text that says: *Click here to reserve your place in paradise.* Another piece of clickbait junk. When I go to swipe it away, my finger accidentally taps the link.

An image of a spinning golden circle appears, followed by a message in cursive: *Welcome, Maxwell Maddison. You have been chosen to join the CIRCLE OF TRUST.*

The message is too personal, not to mention creepy as hell. I close the app and shove my phone into my jeans pocket. I'm starting to hate the internet.

And for the life of me, I can't shake the image of the golden circle spinning in my head. Did I really see that, or am I just so damn dog-tired that I imagined it? ...

... Circle of trust ...

A vivid memory rises to the surface: a finger, describing a circle in the air. A despicable voice from the bloody past saying, *"Do you know what this is, Maxwell?"*

I get this dull, dark pain in the pit of my stomach. It can't be him. It's just a coincidence, I tell myself. Still, I don't dare to open YouTube again. Instead, I stare at the Zenith's dead screen. In the dim morning light, a small, distorted reflection of me stares back.

What's going on out there in the world?

I know better than to dive into that toxic rabbit hole. Turning on the stupid TV is terrible for my mental health—no question about it. But maybe if I just tune in for a minute ... What's the harm in watching just a little?

I rush toward the TV and twist the power knob to the ON position. The screen displays nothing but black-and-white snow on all the channels. I double-check the connections, and both the power and cable lines seem intact. It must be the rain, I tell myself. Yes, there's a storm, and a tree must have fallen over and taken out the cable. That sort of thing happens all the time around here. Or maybe the bill needs to be paid.

I shut off the Zenith. I ought to forget about the previous two minutes of my life and try to get some sleep. Stupid apps. I'm deleting my YouTube the second I wake up. I mean it.

I've got a couple of hours before Sunshine relieves me from my shift, so I do my best to get comfy on the sofa and begin to count the pitter-patters on the window glass above me: one, two ... skip a few ... ninety-nine, one hundred ... It's coming down hard. My body relaxes and I drift away, feeling lighter by the second, sinking into the sweet darkness of la-la land—

EEEERRRRRROOOOORRRCCCCHHH!

Is that the Jeep's brakes? Sunshine's never back this early. A car door slams and I hear running footsteps, then the front door flies open and Sunshine bolts inside. Mascara is running down her face as if she's been crying; her chest is heaving and her face is pale.

"What's going on?" I ask, jumping up and rushing to her.

Sunshine's hyperventilating. Is someone chasing her? I slide past her to close and lock the door. I haven't seen her so upset since—

"We—we—there's—" she stutters.

"Slow down. Did something happen at the hospital?"

Sunshine shakes her head and grabs both of my wrists. She stares at me wide-eyed and says, her words fast and clipped, "My father—he warned me. We have to go! All of us have to leave. Now, Max!"

Carter storms into the room, yelling, "Some of us are trying to sleep around here! If you don't mind shutting the hell—" His tune changes as he takes in Sunshine's panicked condition. "Cuz, what the hell? What's wrong?"

Sunshine takes a breath and drops her death-grip on my wrists. Then she utters my least favorite words in the English language. "Check the news."

Carter lifts his phone out from his front pocket and taps on it briefly. His eyes reflect the screen's bright glow as he scans, and then his face freezes as if he's seen a ghost.

"What the fuck is it?" I ask.

Carter shakes his head.

"Come on!" I demand.

He shoves his phone in my face, and I glance at the New York Times headline. "Nuh-uh," I say. "Both of you can fuck the fuck off right now! I thought we were past that crap. I'm out of here." I can't believe these two, still trying to punk me even after Carter's fake-ass apology. I start to shake with anger.

"Max!" Sunshine cries. "We're not fucking around!"

"America has been attacked? Mandatory draft? War?" I yell. "Tell me now that this is a sick joke, and I'll forgive you two. Just tell me the truth, goddamnit!"

"This isn't a joke, brother!" Carter says.

There's that word, the one word that pierces

through my heart without fail every time he says it —*brother*.

REEE! REEE! REEE! REEE!

Siren-like shrieks erupt—all three of our phones are going off, flashing emergency alert texts and emitting ear-splitting alarms.

EFFECTIVE IMMEDIATELY, ALL ELIGIBLE INDIVIDUALS MUST REPORT TO REGISTER FOR THE DRAFT!

PRESIDENTIAL ALERT: A NATIONAL EMERGENCY HAS BEEN DECLARED! FOLLOW OFFICIAL UPDATES AND PREPARE FOR IMMEDIATE ACTION!

U.S. DEFENSE ALERT! MISSILE ATTACK AT JOINT BASE ELMENDORF-RICHARDSON! MORE MISSILES IN ORBIT! SEEK SHELTER AND STAY INDOORS!

"Fuck ... you're serious," I mutter. My knees feel like they've turned into Jell-O. The world is spinning out of control, and I feel it pulling me away with it ... *breathe, Max.* Then I feel Sunshine's hand on my arm guiding me to the sofa. She nestles herself on the cushion next to me and pats my back as I steady my breath.

The emergency alerts are overriding our phones. "Shut up!" Carter screams as he hurls his phone across the room. "What are we going to do, huh? What the *fuck* are we going to do?!" he rages over and over like a loon. "What the fuck is going on? I'm serious—WHAT THE HELL? This is some sick nightmare, right? I'm hallucinating all of this! I slipped into a coma in the pit after falling face first into that dead man's hairy ass cheeks!"

I haven't seen him this wound up since the day that Phase Zero was announced. He's pacing like a caged animal, scratching his head and leaving red streaks across his prematurely bald dome. I'm tempted to make a crack at him in revenge for his earlier prank—*"That's a nice march, soldier, you sure look ready for the front lines!"*

Carter starts messing with the television, cursing as he flips through the fuzzy channels. "Fuck me sideways! Why isn't this stupid piece of shit working? Has the entire world fucked itself or what?" He goes all Joe Pesci on the Zenith's cabinet, smacking it and yammering, "Come on you little bitch, what do you want? Do you hear me? Huh? Where's the news, asshole? Give it to me or I'll dig you a fucking hole in the ground! Do your job, and nobody gets hurt!"

The emergency alerts finally stop blaring. I wonder out loud, "If this is real and there is a draft, who goes and who stays?"

"Let me see." Sunshine's hands are shaking, but she begins searching on her phone's browser. "Here," she says faintly. "In the Boston Globe."

"Speak up and spit it out!" Carter snaps.

Sunshine flips Carter the bird. "It says here that *any* able-bodied person between the ages of 18 and 26 will have to report to the nearest city hall for an immediate and mandatory physical and mental screening."

"Jesus, we're royally fucked," Carter mutters. "Wait! Max!" He gets a crazy look in his eyes, all crossed and squinted. "Max, you'll get us off the hook. You have ... thanatophobia? Isn't that a serious illness?"

He's correct, but I'm not currently on any meds, nor have I had a professional diagnosis for years. Uncle Sam won't give two shits if a potential soldier has been addicted to light therapy booths for his entire adult life.

"I don't think they'll excuse—"

"Fuck your excuses, Max!" Carter shouts. "Tell them Sunshine and I are your caregivers! That way, we all can—"

"Carter," Sunshine interrupts him, "it also says that any exceptions must be cleared by a military physician regardless of present or past diagnosis or injury."

"Fuck this noise. I'll go freeze my ass off in Canada!"

"I don't think so, Carter," Sunshine says, scrolling on her phone. "It says here in the

Vancouver Sun, Canadian borders are closed until further notice."

"Well ... Mexico it is then! ¡Viva la Revolución! I took Spanish in my junior year. We'll go south—"

"Nope. The U.S.-Mexico border is a no-go. All the borders are closed. Nobody is getting out of here unless you climb that stupid wall."

Carter's eyes bug out and his lips curl into a deranged smile. "Damnit! We're trapped like fucking rats on a sinking ship. Over my dead body would I serve. Sonofafuckingbitch—fuck fuck fuck fuck!"

"Son! What's with all the commotion? Take that crap outside!" Chuck limps into the room and surveys us, frowning. We don't say a word, but an atmosphere of panic and fear lingers in the living room like a nerve gas. Chuck's expression softens as his attention locks on his niece's tear-streaked face. "What's going on, sweetie?"

Carter blurts out, "The U.S. has been attacked, and now there's a mandatory draft!"

Chuck's head whips toward his son, then back toward Sunshine. "Is that true?"

Sunshine nods. "I'm afraid so, Uncle Chuck."

"Well then," Chuck says, puffing up his chest. "Sounds like we'd better get ourselves ready, don't we?"

"Ready for what, Chuck?" I ask nervously. Is

he about to tell us that we're a bunch of sniveling babies, and that we better get ready to serve our country just like he did?

"The way I see it," Chuck says, "we run. No way am I letting this country take more of my family from—" He grabs his gut and lets out a whimper. He staggers over to the La-Z-Boy and eases into it.

"Uncle Chuck," Sunshine cries. "Are you okay?"

"I'm fine, sweetie. Don't you worry about a thing."

The memory of Chuck's rotting flesh floods my mind. "He is far from fine!" I say. "Forget the draft—Chuck needs to see a doctor!"

"What's up with Pops?" Carter asks.

"He has a serious infection, that's what's up! I saw it, and I re-wrapped him last night."

"What? Uncle Chuck, haven't you been taking your medicine?" Sunshine rushes to his side.

Chuck pats her hand. "There's no need to worry about me, sweetie. Let me worry how to get you three the hell out of Dodge before you're all sworn into the Corps. This isn't my first rodeo, and I know a thing or two about how the military works. They're not going to take you out of your home in the middle of the day. The military is as slow as molasses! We have time. Now, let's put our heads together and come up with a plan." He suddenly winces and clutches his gut with both hands.

"Uncle Chuck, I'm taking you to St. Joseph right now," Sunshine says, her hands curling into fists. "Damnit, I wish I still had my aloe medicine. That would fix you right up."

Ding!

My phone chimes, and it's not an emergency alert this time. It's a text message that reads: *It's me Crutch. Get out of there NOW! Meet me at 74 W 3rd St, Falls.* Great. Of all the places in the world, he wants us to meet him on his home turf—fucking Oak Falls.

"Guys, it's Crutch," I announce. "He says we have to meet up with him right now."

"Tell that carrot top we don't have time to deal with his kindergarten shit!" Carter snaps. "There's a war and a fucking draft and my Pops needs help!"

Ding! Another text message comes in. I read out loud, "Hurry, running out of time."

"Yeah, no shit, we're running out of time," Carter says. "That kid's head is thick as—"

BAM! BAM! BAM!

Someone's hammering at the door. The four of us freeze and stare at each other.

"Did someone order a pizza?" Carter whispers.

A voice inside my head screams, *"RUN!!!"*

BAM! BAM! BAM!

"This is Lieutenant Peterson! I've got a draft notice from Uncle Sam! Now, be an obedient citizen and open the fucking door before I break it down!"

Chuck presses a finger against his lips. "Nobody move," he whispers. "He's bluffing."

BAM! BAM! BAM! BAM!

The banging doesn't let up, accompanied by screams of "Open up!" The door jamb begins to splinter inward.

"Who's got my Jeep keys?" Chuck whispers.

Sunshine pulls them from her pocket and holds them up.

Chuck gets to his feet. "Hold on to those, sweetie. Kids, we're going out the back, on the double! That door won't hold forever!"

13. ON WITH THE SHOW

I'll tell you what, it's been a ball-buster of a day. Junior and the entire Holtz clan—Holtz and his wife Louise, their twin boys Todd and Rex, and their little girl Beth—arrived early this morning, but there wasn't much time to catch up because Holtz wasn't looking so well. Without wasting a precious minute, Doc put him under for his much-needed liver transplant.

I won't keep you in suspense—Holtz's surgery was a great success. He's recovering now in the west wing suite of the church. After a liver transplant, most people need a full day of rest or more, depending on age and surgical technology used. But Doc smothered his surgical wound with the aloe medicine, and the remarkable elixir speeds up the healing process tenfold, maybe even more.

Doc's been working his ass off, chipping away at our growing family of essentials. The initial trickle became a flood, and newcomers have been by the hundreds every hour. With Samantha's help, Doc programmed a dozen essentials to perform the procedure themselves, exponentially increasing our productivity. Thousands of lost souls are processed by now, but there's still a shit-ton more to go.

I left Samantha in charge of checking in new arrivals. She's a quick learner, and I trust she's doing a brilliant job—I have no choice, because I need time to prepare my sermon.

As the saying goes, first impressions last forever, and that's especially true for freshly chipped brains. They'll suck up whatever I tell them during their first day post-surgery, so my presentation must go off without a hitch. I've been rehearsing my script in my dressing room, facing a full-length mirror, making certain that I have my delivery down pat.

Your image is crucial when speaking to a crowd—how you look, how you hold yourself. It's just as important as the words leaving your mouth. As I admire my reflection, I can say I look like someone who knows what the fuck he's talking about.

I mean seriously, hot damn mama, look at me! Who could resist someone dressed in such exquisite threads, with such perfect hair like *moi?* Nobody! And don't forget my most prized asset: my irresistible, full-toothed CEO grin. My fuckin' grin should be illegal because it's going to melt minds. Jim, you are one charming son-of-a-gun—that's for certain.

After an hour of practicing in the mirror, I have my smirk down like a boss, and I'm ready for the next phase of my life to unfold. Forget Phase Zero, Jim. This go-around will be different. Fuck the past; the future is what I give a shit about.

Project Exodus is nearing its culmination, and I can already feel its electrifying energy. My essentials and I will soon watch in peace while fear and chaos engulfs the rest of the pathetic world. How those fools will wish they could have joined me!

Now, where was I? Oh, yes ... my sermon.

"Jim! Can you hear me? Jim!"

It's Doc's voice, sounding frazzled through my wireless earpiece. Doc, Junior, Samantha, and I are each rocking one of these, along with lavalier mics clipped to our shirts and set to a private communication channel.

"This better be good, Doc. I'm in the middle of something."

"Yes, of course. This is extremely important, Jim. Junior tells me that the MPV is MIA!"

Doc's words sink like daggers into my gut.

"Are you a hundred fucking percent positive, Doc? Why isn't Junior telling me this shit?"

"Umm, I don't know, he told me then ran off ... Jim, I gotta tell you, I can't think straight ... I've been at it since last night without a wink of sleep ... I've had to process so many essentials ..."

Doc is going to crack. I can't have that happen on my watch. I stand up straight, checking myself out again in the mirror—looking at my handsome figure calms me down—and I tell him, "Tell you what, Doc, go take a nap. You've earned it. You're going to need your strength as we approach the finish line. Now, unless there's anything else, I'll be getting back to business."

"Well ..." Doc says, lost for words.

"Well, what now, Doc?" I watch in the mirror as my pale complexion transforms to a shade of blood-red right before my eyes.

"Well, our sewer rat ... he might have gone rogue, Jim. He's not responding to any communication."

"Christ almighty!" I scream.

That worthless little bastard fucked me. I'm so pissed off, I could slam my fist through the wall, but instead, I smooth my hair and flash myself a suave grin in the mirror. That's better. Now, time to get my wheels back on track.

"Forget the MPV and screw that no-good rat,

got me, Doc? On with the show! Nothing changes; it will go just as we planned before. Oh, and Doc —forget that nap! Get your wrinkled old ass in gear and finish off the rest!"

14. WHERE THERE'S SMOKE

Sunshine and I jam our shoulders into Chuck's armpits, and we move together as fast as humanly possible toward the back door, one clumsy step at a time. Carter leads the way.

I'm struggling to keep Chuck on his feet. We're close now—through the kitchen, past the dining room table, and just as we slip out through the back, I hear the front door shatter into pieces behind us—KA-BASH! Lieutenant Peterson has breached the building.

Lucky for us, we're already outside, but there's no time to celebrate. The Jeep sits some fifty paces around the corner, and the sky is dumping down cold Cascadian buckets of rain. Within seconds, we're all soaked and shivering as we slide around the house toward our getaway vehicle.

As we sneak past a side window, I glimpse

Peterson tearing through the house with his flashlight and pistol. He's a burly dude in a green uniform, and for someone as big as he is, he's quick on his feet. It's just a matter of time before he realizes we're not inside.

Carter dashes ahead to the Jeep and slides in behind the driver's seat. "Hurry the fuck up, you three!" he hisses at us.

"Go on without me—I'm slowing you down," Chuck mumbles.

"Shut up," Sunshine grunts in between breaths. "One foot in front of the other, you hear me?"

We reach the Jeep, and on the count of three, we hoist Chuck into the passenger seat next to Carter. Sunshine runs around and climbs in behind the steering wheel, and I scramble into the shotgun seat. She fires up the engine.

An instant later, Peterson's flashlight beam slices through the rain, sweeping toward us. He stands silhouetted in the splintered frame of the front door, glaring out at us.

"Step on it, Sunshine!" I yell.

The Jeep lurches backward down the driveway. "Hold onto your butts!" Sunshine says, wrenching the wheel. The tires screech as we peel out, leaving Peterson behind in the pre-dawn darkness.

"Shit, I forgot my phone!" Carter moans.

"Who cares?" Sunshine snaps. "What's important is that we got away from that maniac, with no one left behind."

No one left behind ... Which reminds me— "Crutch!" I yell. "We have to go get him!" Even if that means we have to visit my least favorite place on Earth.

Chuck says, "I'm there with ya, Max. We gotta go get the little guy."

"Pops, we need to get you to a doctor!" Carter protests.

"Don't you worry about me. I know a great walk-in clinic out there. The Falls is practically on the way."

For once, Carter doesn't argue, and Sunshine points the Jeep toward the Falls. After taking a roundabout at forty miles an hour, she steers us onto the Mount Baker Highway Northbound.

Early morning fog swirls on the highway. It's near dawn, but with the fog and the thick clouds overhead, it might as well be the middle of the night. The northbound lane is packed with motorists. All the vehicles seem to be crammed with supplies, tarp-covered loads piled high on rooftops and stuffed into truck beds. I'd guess they're trying to escape to their off-grid doomsday bunkers before they either get drafted or blown to bits by missiles.

We inch up the highway for a few miles at the

speed of a snail's crawl. Sunshine flips on the radio, and a newscaster's voice fills the cab:

"—the initial attack on American soil, we've just received intel that three additional nuclear-capable stealth rockets have been launched into orbit. The source of the attack is still unclear, and the targets remain unknown. However, the Pentagon confirms that America is already preparing for war. In related news, the first mandatory U.S. military draft since 1973 began this morning. Thousands have already been conscripted and shipped out, while others have—"

"CUZ!" Carter yells over the radio.

"Hundreds of thousands of protestors have started picketing state capitol buildings across the country—"

"What do you want, Carter?"

"There have been over six hundred arrests in Seattle alone as the country has been—"

"Turn it off! Come on, we need some peace and quiet back here."

"At KOMO 16 News, we're here to bring you the latest—" Click. Static replaces the newscaster's voice.

"Thank you," Carter says.

"I didn't do anything. It cut out on its own," Sunshine replies. She turns the radio off, muting its static. All I hear now is the rumbling of the

Jeep's engine and the whir of its wheels over the wet road.

"Well, it's off, at least," Carter says. "Pops fell asleep, so let's keep it down."

Sunshine and I glance at the back seat, and it's true—Chuck's eyes are shut, and he's slumped over.

"He's just sleeping, right?" Sunshine asks nervously.

Carter lays two fingers against the side of his father's throat. A few seconds later, he says, "Yeah, don't worry, cuz."

"Everyone else doing okay? Max? Carter?"

"Yes," we chorus.

The concern in Sunshine's voice reminds me of one thing I've learned from the recent fiasco—while my friends might not be related to me by blood, they're my family, and we take care of each other. Never mind the occasional prank; when the shit hits the fan, we've got each other's backs.

The other thing that I've learned is that when the world goes bonkers, it's best to keep calm and rely on your instincts. That voice in your head, listen to it—it's speaking to you for a good reason. Most people ignore their inner voice; they're unaware of it, or choose to be stubborn assholes. Or they hear so many other voices that it gets drowned out.

Sunshine's voice must be telling her to drive

fast, to distance ourselves from Peterson. She's finding gaps in the traffic and weaving the Jeep around slow-moving cars, even driving onto the shoulder when necessary. I've never seen her handle a car like this before.

"Nice driving, Steve McQueen," I say, but nobody gets it. "Bullitt? Anybody?" No response from either of the cousins, and that's okay. It's their loss that they missed out on one of the most iconic car chases in cinematic history. I glance at Sunshine, hoping for a smile at my quip, at least.

"Hey, Sunshine," I say.

She keeps her eyes fixed on the road ahead. The raindrops on the windshield cast strange shadows on her face. "What's up, Max?"

Maybe I picked the wrong time to ask—those rain-shadows could be tears—but seeing that I already have her attention, there's no reason to stop. I continue, keeping my voice a decibel above a whisper. "Earlier, you said that your father warned you. ... warned you about what?"

Sunshine is silent for a moment. Then she says, "My father was drafted for the Vietnam War when he was eighteen, two years after Uncle Chuck."

"I didn't know your father was in Vietnam too."

"Why would you know?" Sunshine says

sharply. "Sorry." She bites her lower lip. "My father would never talk about it to anybody."

"Why not?"

"Something happened to my father over there. ... I don't know what, but what I do know from my mother is that after he came home, he became an anti-war protestor. That's how they met, at a street rally in Seattle. Growing up, I saw what the military did to my father. He refused to talk about it, but he'd have these night terrors. I remember him screaming—"

HONK!

Sunshine lays down on the Jeep's horn and swerves onto the shoulder to avoid a brake check. She speeds up, smoothly cuts ahead of the offending vehicle, then continues as if nothing happened. "I can't imagine what kind of hell he went through, what kind of pain he had to endure, all because of a draft that forced him to fight in a war he didn't believe in. In a way, it always made me feel like I never got to know the real him."

I think back to when I was at her house before it got torched by Jim's goons, remembering the framed Sears family portrait that I saw there. They seemed happy in the photo, but now I imagine her as a little girl, trying to connect to a distant, damaged father.

Sunshine keeps talking, as if an inner floodgate has opened. "Anyway, that's what I meant when I said he warned me. My father made me promise that I would never enlist in the services, no matter what. I didn't understand why when I was little, but when I grew up, I realized he wanted to protect me. He was a good guy, a great father." Then she reaches over to pat my knee and says, "He would have liked you, Max."

"Thanks." I want to say more, but I'm at a loss for words. She's never shared this much with me before. Like I said, we've barely ever had a personal conversation.

As if a switch flipped, I'm looking at her in a new light, and our relationship too. I'm just glad to be here for her, as someone she can talk to. She's a wonderful person: kind, smart, beautiful inside and out. I'm lucky to have a friend like her in my life. Jeez, what was I thinking earlier? Friend zone? I should be honored to be her friend.

"What the fuck is that?" Carter yells from the back. Sunshine pulls her hand back into her lap and redirects her attention to the road. We're more than halfway to the Falls by now, and traffic's cleared up.

"What's what, son?" Chuck asks, startling awake.

"I don't know," Carter says. He's got his nose glued to the rear window. "It looks like a dump truck, and it's coming in hot!"

Carter's right. Approaching behind us is a

large vehicle with its high beams on. It could be a dump truck, but I've never seen one move so fast.

A voice from a PA system booms, "This is the United States Military. Pull over, now!"

Chuck yells, "Crap, it's an MPV!"

"A what? English, Pops!"

"It's a military patrol vehicle," Chuck explains. "Put your blinker on for now. But whatever you do, don't pull over, Sunshine!"

Sunshine smacks the turn signal lever, and the Jeep's amber blinker flashes through the blanket of fog. "What now, Unc—"

KA-BAM!

The MPV collides with the Jeep's bumper, causing us all to jerk forward and the Jeep to jolt to the side. Carter says *fuck* about twenty times, Sunshine screams, and Chuck shouts for her not to pull over. Sunshine corrects our course and stomps on the gas pedal. For a second, I think we're in the clear.

KA-BAM!

We're hit again. My teeth rattle in my skull from the collision, and I grab the oh-shit bar by my head with both hands. Sunshine miraculously keeps the Jeep steady and picks up the pace. The speedometer needle climbs to 60, 70. ... "What's the plan, guys?!" she screams.

"I'm gonna check GPS," I tell her. "Hopefully there's an exit coming up."

The PA booms again, "Pull your vehicle over!" KA-BAM!

Sunshine jerks the wheel back and forth, trying to prevent the Jeep from spinning out of control. I release one hand from the oh-shit bar and fish for my cell—got it. I pull up a map, but there's a big fat slash through the network icon. "My network is down!" I yell. "I can't use my GP—"

KA-BAM!

My phone flies out of my hand and smacks against the Jeep's windshield.

"PULL YOUR VEHICLE OVER!" The high beams behind us are joined by a set of emergency lights, flashing red and white.

Carter screams, "Like hell, we will! Fuck this guy!"

Sunshine floors it. The Jeep's engine growls as we climb to eighty miles per hour. In the rearview mirror, the MPV's lights are close behind us.

"This Jeep needs to rock 'n' roll off-road!" Chuck hollers.

"Guys, the windshield is fogging up! I can barely see!" Sunshine cries.

"Dang, the heater must be on the fritz again," Chuck says. "I knew I should have had that fixed."

"Can someone help me out?" Sunshine pleads. "Do you see any exits?"

That's when I'm struck with an idea. I roll

down my window and straighten my legs, shoving half of my body outside into the torrential rain. I grab the oh-shit bar again, this time with my left hand, twisting my torso until I'm facing forward.

"What the hell are you doing, Max?" Carter cries. Ignoring him, I shield my eyes with my right forearm and squint, searching for an escape route. But there's nothing—no logging road, no turnoff, just a thick wall of trees butted up against the highway shoulder as far as I can see.

"Max! Get back inside!" Chuck yells. "You're gonna get yourself killed!"

I don't give a shit. If we don't shake this bastard, we're done for. I peer straight ahead, my focus steady like a lookout in a ship's crow's nest.

We skid around a bend. Up ahead, I see electric towers rising up on either side of the highway, cables extending between them. Lights from the towers illuminate a hillside to our right. I recognize it! When we were younger, Carter and I used to ride his ATV out here through a bunch of service roads—his idea, not mine. I always thought that thing was a death trap.

I lower myself back inside the cab. "Sunshine, see those lit-up towers up ahead?"

She leans forward to wipe condensation from the windshield with the back of her hand. "Yeah, I—"

KA-BAM!

The Jeep's tires squeal as they skid on the road, careening into the oncoming lane and causing me to collide with Sunshine's shoulder. We spin once, twice—I lose count—then come to a stop. I peel myself off Sunshine and raise my head. Through the windshield, I'm looking straight into the grill of the MPV and its blinding headlights, towering over our Jeep. Next to it, a broad-shouldered figure stands in the rain —shit, it's Peterson! He steps toward us, sidearm drawn.

"Sunshine!" I yell. But she doesn't respond. I look over to see that she's slumped over, her head resting on the steering wheel.

"Get the fuck out of your vehicle now!" Peterson barks. He's by Sunshine's door, face shadowed by the brim of his cap. He lifts his handgun and taps the window glass with the butt end of the weapon.

Sunshine comes to with a gasp, tossing back her ponytail as she straightens from the steering wheel. Peterson smashes through the glass with his pistol and grabs Sunshine's shoulder.

"All of you, you're coming with me!"

"Fuck you, man!" Carter yells. "I have rights!"

"Over my dead body!" Sunshine cries, then chomps down on Peterson's hand. He yelps in pain and instinctively tries to pull away, but she hangs on tight.

"Let go, you bitch!" Peterson howls. He raises the gun in his free hand.

Sunshine obeys, then pulls the door latch. With a swift kick, she slams the door into Peterson, knocking him off his feet.

"Drive!" I scream.

I'm tossed back into my seat and the world outside becomes a blur. The Jeep spins around like a teacup at Disneyland, narrowly missing a car in the oncoming lane. Then we're off, hurling down the highway.

POP! POP!

Bullets ricochet against the Jeep's frame. "Duck and cover!" Chuck cries.

Sunshine and I hunch down and peer up over the dash to view the road ahead. "There!" I say, pointing my finger like the nose of an eager bloodhound. "Turn right at those electric towers! There's a service road. You'll see it!"

Sunshine does, and she veers off the highway onto an unmarked road that's barely more than a deer path. The overgrown road zigzags up the hill, winding through a thin patch of pines. The Jeep's suspension squeaks as we pass one electric tower after another.

Just as I'm about to let out a victory shout, red-and-white strobes in the rearview mirror shut me up.

POP! POP!

Carter shouts, "Fuck me! He's back!"

"Hold on!" Sunshine says, then jams the gas pedal to the floor. But we don't go any faster—the opposite, in fact. The tires spin uselessly, caught on a large rock. The approach angle is too steep, and the surface too slick with mud. "There's no grip," she cries, pumping the brakes as we slide backward—straight toward the approaching MPV!

"Pops!" Carter shouts. "I thought this thing could rock 'n' roll on any road!"

"She can—Sunshine, put her in four-low," Chuck tells her. "Shove it in low gear. Down and over!"

Sunshine slides the 4x4 shifter into gear. "Got it!" She gives the Jeep some gas, and its tires catch traction. We make it over the boulder and keep crawling up the service road.

"Faster, cuz, he's gaining on us!" Carter says.

"You got this, sweetie!" Chuck cheers. "Keep those RPMs up!"

The Jeep fishtails as Sunshine takes a sharp corner without warning. She leans forward as she wrestles with the road. Her knuckles grow white as the Jeep teeters on the edge of stability. I'm convinced we'll tip over, or blow a tire, or worse—

KA-BAM!

We're airborne. Nausea overwhelms me as we're suspended mid-air for an instant, like a roller coaster car at the top of a loop. Then gravity takes hold, and we're plummeting down, down, down. My arms cover my face as I prepare for impact. 3—2—THUD!

The Jeep lands upright, bouncing on all four tires. Sunshine hits the brakes and we skid to a stop.

Behind us, the MPV appears stuck. It's slid off the road and wedged itself between two enormous trees. Its doors are pinned and its tires spin, first forward, then in reverse. Smoke rises from its hood, and last I checked, where there's smoke, there's fire. Sure enough, a tongue of flame appears from beneath the hood. Within seconds, the MPV is engulfed in flames.

None of us can move; we're transfixed by the sight of the burning wreck. None of this feels real. It feels like we're sitting in one of those old drive-in theaters, watching an action movie on a giant outdoor screen. Where's my popcorn?

Lights, camera, action! The MPV's rear door bursts open, and Peterson stumbles out, his uniform ablaze. He rolls on the ground, screaming and clawing at his clothes, trying to tear them off.

KA-BOOM!

The MPV explodes, and Peterson with it.

Chunks of burning flesh and shrapnel rain down, peppering the forest floor and splattering the Jeep with gore.

Cut. End scene.

15. Home Sweet Home

I never imagined that I could feel this way, but I'm thrilled we've made it to the Falls. Just barely. The Jeep's rear tires have gone flat, and its alignment is all out of whack, forcing Sunshine to compensate by keeping the wheel twisted to the left. The engine is wheezing like it's got asthma. But we're making progress, inching forward at a whopping seven miles per hour. Hey, at least the rain let up, making it much easier to see.

Inside the city limits of the Falls, we pass one busted-up trailer after another. Jesus, this stinkin' place is the same as it's always been, maybe worse. Heaps of trash rot on the sidewalks, and packs of flea-bitten stray dogs trot around like they own the joint. But compared to our recent high-speed chase with that psychotic MPV, it's what the town's travel brochure says it is: a slice of heaven.

"Max," Sunshine says, "where did Crutch say to meet him?"

"I'll check my phone," I tell her. I find it lodged against the windshield on the dash. The screen is cracked and it still can't connect to a network, but I can access my old text messages. I tell her. "Seventy-four West Third Street." Just in the nick of time—right as the phone battery runs out of juice and the screen goes black.

As we cruise down Main Street, I don't see a single soul outside. My guess is that the citizens of the Falls are barricaded in their trailers with loaded shotguns, waiting for—no, *wanting* someone like Lieutenant Peterson to come knocking on their doors.

"Looks like this is Third," Sunshine says. We turn onto a potholed dirt road off Main, and shortly after, the Jeep screeches to a halt next to a rusted chain-link fence. Nailed to a crooked post, a piece of plywood displays the spray-painted number 74. A packed dirt driveway runs from the road to a weathered double-wide trailer in the middle of a decent-sized lot.

"I don't see a gate," Sunshine says. She honks the horn and immediately, a ginger head pokes out from the trailer. Crutch jogs out and presses a button somewhere on the fence. A section of the fence that seemed seamless swings open smoothly.

"Slick," Chuck says admiringly.

Crutch waves us through, and the gate shuts behind us. We coast up the driveway and stop close to the double-wide. Before Sunshine can kill the engine, it coughs, rattles, then dies.

Sunshine curses as she twists the key in the ignition. No luck—the Jeep is a goner. We jump out and look over the damage. The MPV sure did a number on it, and the bullets must have sealed the deal. A hole in the engine coolant tank is seeping neon green liquid.

Crutch joins us and asks, "Yikes. What happened here?"

"We ran into a little trouble on the road," Sunshine responds casually.

"A *little*?" Carter says. He runs his fingers over the Jeep's mangled bumper.

Crutch turns to me. "Max, do you have your phone on you?"

"Yeah, but the battery's dead."

"Good. Come with me." He motions with his head toward the front door of the trailer.

We start walking in that direction, but Chuck lets out a pain-filled groan. When I look at him, he's got one hand around his midsection, and the other hand waving at us as if to say, go on. "I'm fine," he says, trying to smile. "Just stiff is all, a cramp." Then he hunches over, his knees shaking as if they're about to fail.

Out of nowhere, Crutch is there to catch him. It's amazing how fast the skinny kid can move, and how much weight he can bear. "Gotcha," Crutch says.

Sunshine slides under her uncle's other arm and asks Crutch, "Do you have any gauze here? I have to re-wrap him."

"I think so," Crutch says. Together, they hobble toward the front door.

Carter and I trail behind them. As I walk, I survey Crutch's front yard. It looks like a forgotten summer BBQ. Rusted poles jut out of the lawn, the remains of a swing set long since fallen over. A round Weber grill lies on its side, choked with weeds. Near it is a wooden picnic table, puke-green from moss and weather-rot.

A faded welcome mat at the front door reads: *Home Sweet Home*—cute in a Pottery Barn sort of cheesy way. But when I enter his trailer, there's nothing sweet about it. I've never seen so much junk packed inside one home. Milk crates and sagging cardboard boxes are stacked up to the ceiling on all sides, blocking the windows and leaving just enough space to squeeze through. And there's a foul smell, sour and stagnant.

In one corner of the living room, it looks like Radio Shack took a giant dump. There's a mountain of electronic parts: cracked CRT monitors tangled with cables, hard drives, circuit boards, power bricks, and other stuff I don't even recognize.

"Flippin' fuck, carrot top!" Carter shouts from somewhere behind one of the towers of junk. "Have you ever heard of spring cleaning?"

Carter can be a dickhead, but he's not wrong. Crutch's *sweet home* is a health hazard.

We follow Crutch through the maze into the trailer's kitchen. Well, to call it a kitchen is a stretch. There's no oven range, dishwasher, or microwave, just a small dorm fridge. A plank of wood serves as a countertop, cluttered with dirty dishes and cans—beans, tuna—and a half-empty tub of Jif peanut butter.

Crutch guides Chuck to a wooden stool, then rummages until he finds a first-aid kit, which he hands to Sunshine. "There's not much here," she says, rifling through the kit. "But I'll see what I can do." She gets to work unwrapping her uncle's dressings.

"Max, over here," Crutch says, beckoning to me. He walks away, stepping over an occupied mouse trap. The pinned rodent is shriveled up like a prune; the trap must have got it weeks ago.

I follow him to an area adjacent to the kitchen, where he's set up a makeshift command station amid more stacks of electronics-filled crates. A dining table has been repurposed as a computer desk, holding up multiple PC towers with transparent enclosures. Inside them, fans spin and drives whir busily.

Crutch sits on a rickety folding chair facing three CRT monitors that are hooked up to the PC towers. One displays a command line interface, another has a bunch of windows with bars and graphs, and the third shows a map of Washington State.

There's so much clutter inside this trailer, I start to feel like I'm in one of those I Spy books. I hear scratching sounds in the walls. Rats?—sure. Squirrels maybe, drawn to a fellow hoarder. I feel dizzy and claustrophobic; I should sit down.

There are no other chairs, and there's no way I'm putting my butt on this filthy carpet. I flip over and empty a plastic crate, then set it by the computer desk. Seated on the crate, I'm eye-level with the monitors, and I notice a small photo frame tucked next to them.

It holds a faded photo of Crutch and his brothers. The image must have been taken a few years ago as Crutch looks younger, maybe nine or ten. They've thrown their arms around each other,

Crutch in the middle and his brothers to either side. Their names are inscribed underneath: Quinn, Simon, Theo.

Shit, the last time I saw either Quinn and Theo, they were getting their heads blown off by that asshole Sheriff Evans. And his dad died from mercury poisoning around the same time, leaving Crutch on his own. No wonder he likes hanging out at Chuck's.

"Max, when did your phone battery die?" Crutch asks.

"Um, just when we got to the edge of town. Why?"

Carter walks over with what looks like Sunshine's cell phone high above his head. "No bars anywhere," he mutters. He swings the phone in the air while wandering around the piles of electronics, his eyes glued to the screen. He looks like a puppet with invisible strings tied to his head and joints, controlled by an almighty puppeteer, which he is in a way—controlled by the cellular network god.

"It's useless," Carter moans, then smacks the phone against his leg and curses under his breath. "No network."

"Good," Crutch says.

"How the fuck is that *good*?" Carter snaps. "Do you even have any idea what's happening outside this shitty-ass town? We've got to know what's going on!"

"You will," Crutch says, calm. "That's why I called. Max, give me your phone."

"Why? I told you, the battery's dead."

"Doesn't matter." Crutch holds his hand out toward me, palm up. "You've been bugged," he says, his tone matter-of-fact.

"What?" Carter exclaims. "Who the hell bugged Max?"

"Someone bugged Max?" Chuck asks from the kitchen. "Ahh, careful, that's tender!" he complains as Sunshine rips off another strip of gauze.

"Sorry, Uncle. You've gotta quit wriggling around."

"I'll show—" Crutch begins to say.

"How would you even know how to debug a phone?" Carter interjects.

Crutch cocks his head to the side and murmurs to me, "Circle of trust, right?"

"Circle of what?" Carter throws his hands in the air and laughs. "Ha! This is fucking perfect. We drove all the way here just to listen to some circle-jerk nonsense! Guys, let's get the fuck out of—"

"Nowhere's safe if his phone is tapped," Crutch says. "So, Max, two options. We can either destroy it, or you can let me wipe it clean. Your choice."

He looks dead serious. I hand the phone over. "Go ahead, wipe it," I tell him.

Crutch connects a cable from the back of his PC to my device, then whacks at his keyboard. The monitors flicker as zeros and ones flood the screens.

OOOOOOOOOOOOOOOOOOOOOOOOOOOOOOOOOOOOOOO

OOOOOOOOOOOOOOOOOIIIOOOOOOOOOOOOOOOOOOO

OOOOOOOOOOOOOIIIOOOIIIOOOOOOOOOOOOOOO

OOOOOOOOOOIIIOOOOOOOOOIIIOOOOOOOOOOO

OOOOOOOIIIOOOOOOOOOOOOOOOIIIOOOOOOOO

OOOOOOOOOOIIIOOOOOOOOOIIIOOOOOOOOOOO

OOOOOOOOOOOOOIIIOOOIIIOOOOOOOOOOOOOOO

OOOOOOOOOOOOOOOOOIIIOOOOOOOOOOOOOOOOOOO

OOOOOOOOOOOOOOOOOOOOOOOOOOOOOOOOOOOOOOO

The monitors go dark. On the central screen, a familiar graphic image fades in: a spinning golden circle—the circle of trust. Below it is the text: *Click here to reserve your seat in paradise.*

"Max, did you accept this invite?" Crutch asks.

"Maybe, I don't know," I mumble, flustered. "I was tired, and it was late, or early—why?"

Crutch's fingers flurry across the keyboard. "Well, if you clicked this bait ... gotcha!"—the spinning circle disappears, replaced by the words REFORMAT IN PROGRESS.

"Okay, carrot top, how do you know about this?" Carter asks, folding his arms across his chest. "This sounds like a bunch of bullshit, if you ask me."

Crutch ignores him and keeps typing away.

"Did you hear me?" Carter growls. "How do you know any of this? Someone's been tracking Max, you say? Sure, and I shit rainbows out my ass."

Crutch doesn't respond, which gets Carter even more stirred up.

"You know what, you're just some dumb fucking kid," Carter says. He gestures at the mess all around us. "I mean, what is all this crap?"

Crutch stops and turns to face Carter. The kid looks different, as if transformed into an older version of himself; his brow cuts inward, and his mouth stretches in a thin line. "Crap? Listen up baldie, I'm Gen Z," he says. "I taught myself the home row keys in my mother's womb. I'm trying to help you guys, so shut up and let me help."

"That-a-boy, Crutch, you tell him!" Chuck hollers from the kitchen.

"Whatever, dude," Carter says, rolling his eyes.

"Crutch," I say. "Who's been tracking me?" I'm afraid I already know the answer.

The kid nods toward the left monitor; its screen is still dark and blank. "I've been tracking some strange activity on the dark web all night. Spyware going out in all directions. I traced the affected IPs and one of them was yours. Check this out." Crutch raises his right index finger to the ceiling. He makes a sound effect like a plane falling from the sky as his finger swoops down toward the keyboard. When his finger touches down on the space bar, he says, "Ka-boom," and a video begins to play on the left monitor.

Sunshine helps Chuck walk over closer to the command station, and we all watch together.

An aerial drone video of a jungle. The drone swoops down into glorious canyons with an aqua-blue river below, then flies up above the cliffs to catch a golden sunset over lushly forested mountains. The gorgeous scenery is accompanied by a horrifying voice that I would recognize anywhere. A voice that has cursed my nightmares with its disturbing falsetto tone. The voice of one of the most despicable humans to have ever walked the Earth.

The voice intones: "Welcome, my precious souls. I hear your cries; I see your pain. But don't despair! You have been chosen to join me in paradise, where I will free you from pain and sorrow."

"That's Jim's fucking voice!" I blurt out.

Carter stares at me, wide-eyed. "No way. J & J

Funeral Jim? That guy sounds like his balls have been cut off."

Sunshine says, her voice shaking, "Max is right. That's him."

The drone video dissolves and becomes a studio two-shot. On the left, dressed in black with his hair covered in ginger wig, is that fucking sonofabitch Jim.

And to the right of that fuckface ... I rub my eyes, making sure I'm seeing this correctly, because sitting beside Jim—

"Max ... is that *your mom?*" Carter gasps.

My brain feels as if a chainsaw has just severed a main vein.

The woman on the screen parts her lips to speak. "My name is Samantha. My partner and I invite you to join us this full moon at the Church of the Holy Desert in Snake Bend, Arizona. Join us, and together we'll live in peace and harmony. Join us, and become an essential part of a bright new future."

With a sinister grin, Jim says, "See you in Snake Bend for your initiation. This is goodbye—not forever, but for now."

The video cuts, leaving me stunned.

"That was Mrs. Maddison, all right!" Chuck says.

Sunshine says, sounding excited, "Wait, that means she's not dead!"

"Crutch!" Carter yells. "What the fuck? Are you messing with—"

BUZZZZZZ!

A violent vibration erupts from one of the PC towers. Crutch whips around in his chair and begins typing furiously. His monitors flash white and black, on and off, continuously. He smacks the monitor once, twice with his palm and the flashing stops. Crutch sighs in relief, but then text characters flood his screens. What looks like source code fills his screens, jumbled words and symbols moving too fast for me to comprehend.

"No!" Crutch yells. His fingers blur over the keys as awful crunching sounds emit from his computer. He slams his fists on the keyboard and howls in frustration.

The electricity goes out in the trailer. The PCs, the monitors, the overhead light, everything abruptly shuts off.

In the dark, footsteps pitter-patter across the trailer's floor away from us, followed by the creaking sound of the front door opening. "Hang tight!" Crutch's voice calls out to us, then the door slams shut.

Carter says, "Where the hell does he think he's going?" My eyes adjust; a trickle of sunlight slips through the trailer's windows, casting just enough light to see.

"Son, I'm sure he's just trying to get the power back on."

"And what the fuck was that?" Carter points to the dead monitors. "Max, your mom? She should be dead, but she's alive ... and she's with Jim? This feels bad, so bad ... and how does that little shit know about all this? It doesn't add up. We're just supposed to trust him?"

My head is pounding. I take a deep breath, followed by another. Was that my mother, or was I seeing things? No—Max, don't be an idiot. It's not just me, everyone recognized her. But it sounded nothing like her. Whose voice was that? It sounded oddly familiar.

We hear the sound of a generator turn over, its cylinders puttering until there's a smooth idle. The overhead light comes on, then flickers three or four times before holding steady. The computer towers and monitors remain dark. Crutch rushes inside, moves past Carter, and beelines it toward a pile of boxes. He starts digging through it frantically.

"Christ! This is not the time to go through your shit! Why is everyone so fucking retarded right now?" Carter rages. "Goodness-fucking-gracious, you guys are unbelievable! Wake up! Say something! Have you guys suffered a fucking stroke! FUCK! I'll say the obvious, all of us need to leave this disgusting trailer and go rescue Max's mom from Jim!"

"Carter's right! Let's go find Mrs. Maddison!" Sunshine cries.

"Got it," Crutch says, holding up a keyring full of keys.

"What's that?" Sunshine asks.

"We gotta get out of town, right?"

"And those keys are going to help us do that, huh?" Carter says. "Keys to what? Your stupid bike lock, is that it, Crutch? We'll just pedal to Arizona, all of us on your fucking Schwinn?"

"No. That would be stupid. They're keys to the bus."

Bus? I'm struck by a memory. *I'm with Carter, standing in the middle of a back road near the Falls because there's a school bus parked sideways, blocking both ways of traffic.*

"What *bus* are you talking about?" Carter snaps.

... a diesel Ford truck pulls up alongside my Beast. A man, a ginger-haired mullet hick, climbs down from the driver's seat and says, " ... you fellas are in some good fortune—"

"My dad's bus is parked out back," Crutch says.

A trio of kids emerge from the truck. Mr. Mullet is standing at the rear of his Ford, telling Carter and me, "See here, I got me this winch a while back. Best dang money I ever spent. You wouldn't believe the stuff I had 'er yank ... trees ... boulders ... even a goddamn school bus—

I glance over at Carter, and his face tells me that he doesn't recall that night with the bus, the night we first met Crutch. Frankly, I don't want to be the one to remind him. He can figure that one out on his own.

"Great work, kid," Chuck says. "Well, gang, looks like we're due for a road trip. Next stop: Arizona."

16. MICHAEL AND HIS MOONWALK

It's time to show 'em what you're made of, Jim, you handsome sonofabitch! I'm ready, well-groomed, dressed head to toe in my finest black threads. Steve Jobs, eat your rotting heart out—today's spectacle will put your 2007 iPhone release party to shame.

An electronic crackle in my earpiece makes me jump. "Boss, two minutes," Junior tells me.

I hold down a button on my lavalier mic to activate it. "Roger that," I reply.

From backstage, I peel back a red velvet curtain to gaze out upon what I've accomplished in such a short time. I've created something so unprecedented, so powerful, so glorious that the mere sight brings tears of joy to my eyes.

Before me, I see thousands of lost souls who have joined here together from all corners of this country, seeking a new path. They're now reborn and possess a clear and pure mind, unclouded by doubts and worries.

Now, I must tip my hat to Doc and give him the well-earned credit he deserves for chipping away all through the day. I'm impressed with his efforts. In turn, the Holtzes are impressed with my diligence in executing Project Exodus. Holtz even gave me an appreciative pat on the back earlier. I needed that gratitude, the recognition that his boy Jim has done a good job.

It's a shame that the Holtzes can't be here for this grand reveal. Holtz needs more time to heal before we depart for paradise, and Louise and his children have stayed glued to his side.

I sneak another peek through the curtains. Christ Almighty, would you look at this joint—it's packed! A warm, tingling sensation courses through my veins, and I love it.

This is what God must have felt after creating the universe. They say that He separated the light from the dark, sky from the sea, brought forth all the creatures on this earth, and finished with His masterpiece, His people. And it was then, and only then, that He rested on the seventh day, exalting in His creation.

Yes! I too have created, but unlike God, I shall not rest on the seventh day. Oh no, no rest for me, for there is still much to do today, tomorrow, and the day after that. But I say, good! Bring it on and pile it on thick, because it's true what they say—work never feels like work if you love what you do. And baby, I'm loving every minute of this!

"Jim, you ready?" Junior's voice booms through my earpiece, making me wince.

"Ready? I was born ready. Cue the music, Junior—and turn the volume down on your damn mic!"

A snare drumroll thunders from the auditorium's speakers, slow at first, then building faster and faster until the curtains glide apart. I raise my hands high above my perfectly coiffed hair and strut toward the podium, waving at my essentials and flashing them my dazzling CEO grin. I grab the PA mic from the podium. "Stand up and let me hear you make some noise!" I shout.

And in return, they stand and scream—my essentials cheer their fucking lungs out as if it's Jackson's Bad World Tour from '87—I'm bad, I'm bad, come on, you know I'm bad. But fuck Michael and his moonwalk; this moment is a thousand times more historical than MJ's silly fancy-foot-dance horseshit.

After I've had enough excitement, I hush the roaring crowd with a single word: "Silence."

You could hear a pin drop in the auditorium.

These 2.0 chips that Doc and Samantha designed are marvelous. They're backward compatible with transmitter commands like the 1.0s, but these new ones respond to imprinted voice control as well, preventing another situation like the Evans shitshow.

Evans ... that turd-for-brains sheriff had one job to do, and he screwed it up by losing control of our essentials and our fucking transmitter—fuck! Rot in jail, Evans! Rot in jail and think about how you ruined our entire fucking plan, you and that nitwit dipshit Maxwell and his friends! Rot in jail, you fat fuck!

Shit, get it together, Jim. You're on stage. They're all looking at you.

I clear my throat.

"Sit!" I say, and my essentials take their seats like obedient school children. Now it's time to begin.

"I am Jim, and I'm so happy to have you all here with me. I welcome you from the depths of my heart," I tell them, my voice gentle. Then like the snares, I gradually crescendo, louder and louder, just like I practiced.

"You, my flock, have come to me to be healed. You have come to be uplifted of your suffering. But I'm here to tell you, you do not suffer due to your inadequacy. No! You live in a sick world, and it makes you sick! Sick with worry about the future, sick with grief for the past, sick from being fed poison into your body and soul!"

I pause for breath, panting.

"But now that you're here, you don't have to worry anymore. You don't have to go hungry anymore. I am here to protect you and to guide you to paradise. And you know what? They've been lying to you. You don't have to die to go to heaven. In our paradise, every day will be heaven. You will have your heaven here and now! This is our destiny, and nothing can stand in our way! Let me hear you cheer!"

The auditorium explodes with applause, shaking the holy sanctum. My heart has never felt so full.

"Is that what you want? To become an essential part of a new and glorious world?" I call out, lifting my arms like an orchestra conductor.

In unison, the auditorium responds, "Yes, Jim!"

"In return, all I ask of you is that you listen to me and heed my guidance. I shall lead you into the light! What will you do?"

"We will listen to you, Jim!"

Amazing. I smile, softening my voice again.

"Tell me, my precious essentials—how are you feeling today?"

"We are fantastic, Jim!"

"Damn right you are, you're fan-fuckin'-tastic!"

"We are fan-fuckin'-tastic, Jim!"

"I can't hear you!"

"WE ARE FAN-FUCKIN'-TASTIC, JIM! WE ARE FAN-FUCKIN'-TASTIC, JIM!"

Thousands of mouths screaming my name in adoration.

"Fan-fuckin'-tastic to hear," I tell them, sniffling a little. "I'm so proud of every one of you!"

I've never felt this feeling before. *Proud.* This must be how a father feels after spending years teaching his offspring how to behave. Yes, I'm proud like a father. Wait—that's it! Why haven't I thought of this before?

"My beloved essentials, now hear me say that from this moment forward, you will address me not as Jim, but as Father! Do you understand?"

In unison, they begin to chant, "We understand, Father, we are here to serve and obey! We understand, Father, we are here to serve and obey!"

I think I'm going to have a heart attack. Is this what love feels like? If my fucking ex-wife Jane could see me now! Ha! Look at me; I have thousands of devoted children who would, in the blink of an eye, throw themselves into the path of a bullet to protect me. Me, Jim, their Father, their savior!

My essentials continue chanting. Their words are music to my ears, melting away my pain and fueling my will to succeed. To think of all the struggles to get here, the agony I felt in Bellingham when I lost everything I worked so hard to achieve! This moment, *this*, is more than worth all that bullshit!

"We understand, Father, we are here to serve and obey!"

Yes! I am Father to these essentials, to these once-lonely souls who had no one to turn to, until today, until *me!* Now my circle of trust is enormous! I'm ecstatic inside, and yet, I keep my outward composure. I'm a pro, born to lead.

"Silence!" I roar, and the room quiets once more. "As part education and part entertainment, I have something remarkable to share with you today. You will watch as the world of the nonessentials outside these walls shatters. And as we watch their weak minds break, their pain will become our strength. It will teach you the difference between who they are, and who *you* are. You are the chosen! You are my essentials!"

I stride to the edge of the stage, gracing them with another CEO grin.

"The nonessentials, with their electronic devices glued to their faces—fools they are! We will watch these electronic sheep choke on their own filth! Watch them consume their digital feeds until their devices flatten them with a tidal wave of misinformation that destroys their sinful world! And we shall rise like the mythical phoenix out of its ashes! Together we're going to make earth great again! You're the chosen ones! Angels in my kingdom! Tell me, what are you?"

"FATHER, WE ARE ANGELS! ANGELS IN YOUR KINGDOM!"

I raise my index finger to trace a circle in the air, beaming proudly as the crowd before me mirrors my gesture. "Yes, my essential angels. You are now part of my circle, the circle of trust!" I place my hand across my chest. "Our bond will never be broken! Now, who wants to watch some entertainment on the big screen?"

"WE DO, FATHER! WE DO!"

I notice that the first row of essentials appears less enthusiastic—perhaps they need to be recalibrated. But the cheering of the rest, thousands of voices raised in praise of me, generates an electric energy. I can feel that energy soaking through my skin, seeping into my bones, invigorating my soul. And standing there on that stage before my worshipful flock, I realize what I am. I am a God! Jane, you bitch, look at me now!

"Now, my children, feast your eyes on this!"

17. Away from the What-Ifs

The four of us follow Crutch closely like spring ducklings, leaving his trailer and heading into his backyard. It looks like a Pic-n-Pull out there: heaps of auto parts scattered around several rusted cars, most of them jacked up on cinderblocks.

Crutch stops at a monstrous object shrouded in weather-faded blue tarps. We help him pull off the tarps, revealing the old school bus with its matte-black paint job. It's the Falls' roadblock, straight out of my haunting memory.

Since that night, I've wondered if my life would have turned out differently if we had never tried to take the shortcut through the Falls. If we hadn't, we wouldn't have run into Crutch and his family of miscreants, we wouldn't have got robbed and maced by them, and a lot would have been different after that. Maybe I wouldn't have gotten arrested and ended up working for Jim. Then Sunshine would have never been kidnapped and chipped. Maybe my mom would still be alive.

And maybe Carter is right. Can we trust Crutch?

Carter scans the bus and places his hands on his hips. He looks as if he's connected the dots. "Holy shit, I remember this fucking thing. Crutch, you mace-spraying punk. I still can't believe you and your family pulled that crap on Max and me!"

"Cool it, son," Chuck says, "He's already apologized since, haven't you, Crutch?"

"Well, maybe I want another apology! Maybe I want this little ginger prick to get down on his knees and kiss my shoes and beg for forgiveness, and then, maybe then, I'll accept his—"

"Carter, chill out!" Sunshine snaps. "He's sorry, okay? I've heard him say it half a dozen times, and in case you have forgotten, let me remind you that Crutch has been helping your ass and your father for weeks! Besides, those rolls of toilet paper they took were poisoned anyway, so technically, Carter Jackson, Crutch saved your life."

Carter kicks the ground and crosses his arms over his chest. "Saved my life ... that's fucking rich."

Crutch manages to get the bus's bifold doors

open. He hops up to the first step, then turns around and says, "Carter, Max, I'm sorry. Come on in, guys. There's plenty of room."

"I'll be in soon," Chuck says. "First, I want to give her a look-over."

"I'll be right in too, Crutch," Sunshine says, keeping close to her uncle as he circles the bus, kicking the tires and poking at this and that.

Crutch vanishes into the bus. I follow, with Carter behind me. Up past a set of three metal steps is a padded captain's seat. Facing it is a wide steering wheel wrapped in tan leather, with three worn foot pedals below it and an ancient gear shifter to its side. Mechanical levers litter the wood-veneer dashboard, along with dozens of multi-colored buttons, dials, and gauges. For all the sense I can make out of it, it might as well be the control deck of a submarine or rocket ship.

As I make my way down the aisle, a sharp aroma hits the back of my throat like a sucker punch—the pungent stench of mothballs and motor oil. A nasty combination, but hey, I ran into worse when I worked for J & J Funeral. I shake the thought and pinch my nose shut. If nothing else, the kid wasn't kidding; there's plenty of room inside.

Behind the captain's chair are a half-dozen baby-blue bench seats, arranged in three pairs along the aisle. That's all the seating; the rest have been removed, leaving the rear of the bus empty and spacious. Toward the rear, custom aluminum shelving runs the length of both side walls. The shelving is welded from roof to floor, reminding me of the treatment given my beloved Beast when Jim transformed her into Meat Wagon #4.

"Will someone open a goddamn window?" Carter cries with his nose plugged.

"What do you think?" Crutch asks as we catch up to him at the rear, by the emergency exit door.

"Does it run?" I ask.

"I think so," Crutch replies. He tugs open the emergency exit door, letting fresh air inside.

"You *think* so? You don't know?" Carter barks. "When's the last time it moved? When it was a *roadblock*?" He pushes me aside and steps toward Crutch, his fists clenched.

Oh crap, here we go again. "Carter, relax, man," I tell him.

Carter leans down nose-to-nose with Crutch and says, "So, you don't know if this hunk of metal even runs, is what you're telling me."

I set my hand on Carter's shoulder. "Take it easy, he's just a kid."

"Well, sounds like this *kid* is draining our precious time. Let's get the fuck out of—"

"Here," Crutch says, dangling the bus key in the air. "Try it out yourself."

Carter snatches the key from Crutch's hand,

stomps down the aisle, and takes a seat behind the wheel. "The stupid key won't even turn!" he snaps after a moment. "What's with this hunk of crap?"

"Carter, it's a manual," I say as Crutch and I walk up to join him. "Push in the clutch—that's the pedal left of the brake—then twist the key."

"Left of what brake? Jesus, you telling me now this is a fucking manual? And look at this dash! What the hell is all this? Who's going to drive this piece of junk? No radio? No heat?"

"I am," Chuck says, stepping inside the bus. "Stand aside, son, let your old man take it from here. I'm driving Miss Daisy."

Carter moves aside for the big guy. Chuck lowers himself onto the captain's seat, the springs squeaking as they settle from his weight. He tests the horn, adjusts the rearview mirror, and inspects the dashboard. With a pump of the clutch and a twist of the key, the engine fires right up. He sighs in relief. "She's got a full tank in her."

"Two full tanks," Crutch pipes up. "Diesel, and she gets great miles to the gallon. Dad fixed up her engine."

The bus's engine settles into a deep, throaty hum. Chuck revs the engine again, this time giving it full throttle, and the bus shakes with power. I'm impressed; this vintage clunker sounds like it's got some real pep.

Sunshine boards the bus, frowning at the sight

of her uncle behind the wheel. "So, what about that walk-in clinic you said was out this way, Chuck?"

"Don't you worry about that, sweetie. We can hit up that clinic on the way to Arizona."

"I thought you said it was out here?"

"Sure, it's not far," Chuck assures her. "Guys, we're short on time. We've got to get to Arizona before whatever Jim is planning on the full moon. Every minute we waste here, we're losing a mile, and who knows, there might be another MPV looking for us. Let's get these wheels on the road!" He sounds confident, as strong as I've heard him in ages.

Sunshine says, "Well, how far is Snake Bend from here? I still can't get online. Can you, Max?"

"My phone's still dead."

"My brain isn't," Chuck says. "I used to drive my eighteen-wheeler from Kennewick to Tucson, back in my Teamster days. Snake Bend isn't far west of Tucson. I know the roads between here and there like the back of my hand. I'd say it's about sixteen hundred miles from here, give or take. A little more if we take the back roads to avoid trouble, which we will."

"Sixteen hundred miles!" Carter yells. "How fucking long will that take?"

"Taking the back roads ... over a day, a little

less if I step on it. You got any water or road snacks for the ride, Crutch?"

"Sure thing," Crutch says.

Chuck stays with Miss Daisy to check her vitals, and the rest of us head into the trailer to see what we can scrounge up for supplies. Crutch insists he needs his computer gear, so I help him schlep PC towers, monitors, and milk crates stuffed with parts and tools into the bus. Beside a tangled nest of cables, I notice a bright yellow clamshell lockbox. I lift it and give it a shake. It goes *thud—thud!* Whatever's inside is solid.

"Hey!" Crutch cries. "Be careful with that. It's fragile electronics." He grabs the lockbox from me. "Here, take this out to the bus." He hands me an old IBM laptop.

Meanwhile, Sunshine and Carter have been packing up whatever provisions they can find in Crutch's kitchen, which isn't much: three boxes of Ritz crackers and a tub of peanut butter. I help Carter carry a five-gallon Igloo jug full of Oak Falls well water—the best water in the state, or so he tells me.

Judging by the sun's position, it's about noon by the time we take off in Miss Daisy. Chuck is whistling, happy as a pig in shit to be behind the wheel of a big rig again. To avoid major highways and cities, we take the 9 southbound instead of the I-5.

Though I didn't say anything earlier, I have to admit, I'm not thrilled that Chuck's the one responsible for keeping the rubber on the road. Sure, he's in a jolly mood, but I know for a fact that he's far from one hundred percent healthy—not even close.

I've read that a serious infection can cause a dangerous drop in blood pressure, something called sepsis-induced something-or-another, which can lead a person to lose consciousness. I sit up front and keep my eyes glued on Chuck. If I see his lights go out, you'd better believe I'm diving for that steering wheel.

As we round a bend on the SR-9, I see Chuck raise his hand to grip a chunk of rope dangling above his head. He yanks on the cord, and Miss Daisy's air horn emits a terrifying howl.

AAHHRROOOOGAAA!

"Oorah!" Chuck exclaims. "What a sweet-sounding horn she has on her! Good girl!" Chuck gives the steering wheel a few soft taps, like he's burping a baby.

Is Chuck losing it? I wouldn't describe an obnoxious air horn as sweet—more like nerve-shattering. Maybe the infection has gotten to his brain. I try to calm my nerves. All that matters is that the bus's tires are rolling down the road, and that we're alive, we managed to avoid getting drafted or shot, and our makeshift family is all together again.

Family ... my mother ... the thought of her threatens to send me into shock again—*alive!*—*with Jim!*—so I bury it down deep for now. I'll deal with those thoughts when we get to Arizona. First, we just have to make it there.

AAHHRROOOOGAAA!

"Oorah!"

"Uncle Chuck!" Sunshine calls out from the rear. "Don't get me wrong, I'm thrilled we're on the move, but some of us need to sleep!"

"You bet, sweetie."

"Thank you."

Now it's quiet inside Miss Daisy. Across the aisle, Carter is staring out his window as if he's hypnotized by the trees blurring past us. Sunshine's stretched out in the back, lying on a nest of blankets from the trailer. Surrounded by milk crates on the floor near her, Crutch is tinkering with computer parts.

As the miles and minutes tick past, fatigue drapes over me like a lead blanket. I haven't slept since J & J's, so I've been running on sheer adrenaline since this morning—but that's fading fast. I huddle into the corner of my bench seat and press my head against the cool window glass, trying to get comfortable.

Outside, I count the highway mile markers ...

nine ... ten ... My eyelids flutter as my muscles relax. As I'm about to zonk off, I spot tire skid marks on the road. The rubber skid marks stretch from one mile marker to the next, veering off the shoulder and into a tree that's been split in two. Jammed in the split is a familiar chrome bumper.

In my delirious state, my mind goes crazy. That looked like the bumper of my Beast! It has to be—how could it—who did—my beautiful Beast! I almost scream out, *pull over Chuck! Let me out!*

I calm down by taking a few deep breaths and reminding myself that Sunshine is sleeping. That bumper could have come from any SUV. I've got to keep my mind far away from the what-ifs and the worst-case scenarios, or I'm going to give myself a fucking stroke.

Despite my best efforts, the more I try to relax, the more I can't control the images that flood my head. My mind turns against me, concocting a nightmare I can't escape. I see him—Jim! That Beast-snatching, mother-stealing sonofabitch Jim! He's twirling his finger mid-air in a circle with a shit-eating grin on his face—that greasy-haired fuck!

18. So much swagger

"Hit it!" I command.

The house lights dim. With a grinding of gears, giant white screens lower from the ceiling behind me. Together, the three screens together span as wide as an American football field.

Junior better have got our live feeds in working order. There was no time for a dry run, so there could be any number of technical setbacks, which would be such a buzzkill. I turn to watch in anticipation.

A digital countdown begins on the lower corner of the far-right screen ... 3 ... 2 ... 1 ... show-time! Thousands of horrified faces fill every square inch of the three screens. Yes! All is well with the world. Ha! At least, in *my* world.

Each face is captured by the camera of a smartphone held up by its subject, piped straight from social media livestreams from all over the country as well as private video calls. The thousands of selfie videos look like scenes from the Blair Witch flick—distorted, noses dripping with snot, eyes full of tears as the pathetic nonessentials lose their minds over what they've been seeing on the news. A cacophony of weeping and shrieks from the feeds fills the speakers. After a moment, I tell Junior to lower the audio to a background hum.

My congregation stares blankly at the screens, silently absorbing what they see. All except the first row. They seem disturbed—twitching and fiddling in their seats. Doesn't matter now; the show must go on.

"My children, look upon these sniveling *non*essentials!" I shout. "Look at these morons, consumed by terror, yet see how they do nothing except piss themselves, with their precious devices in their faces! Your blood will never run cold from fear, your brains will never freeze when met with danger, because you are free!"

On the thousands of live feeds behind me, the nonessentials are still sobbing, tearing at their hair, babbling, screaming.

"There's something interesting about a species that doesn't know how to run from danger," I muse into the PA mic. "If an animal sees fire, they scurry. But instead of fleeing to safety, these nonessentials chatter meaninglessly online, liking, sharing, and making pointless comments! They feed on each other's fear, spreading panic, gossip, and *lies!*"

The audio from the live feeds cuts out, and the screens go dark. "What the hell's going on, Junior?" I hiss into my lav mic.

"The satellites—"

"I don't care, just fix it! Meanwhile, Samantha baby, are you listening?"

"Always, Jim."

"I need you in here, pronto!"

I pull the PA mic back to my mouth. "Now, it's time for a round of applause. Allow me to introduce you to the incredible Samantha! Just as you call me Father, you will call her Mother, and pay her the respect she deserves!"

The audience claps enthusiastically as the center projector screen rises, first revealing a pair of navy-blue pumps behind it. Little by little, the retracting screen exposes a woman's figure in a tight navy-blue suit, then her face—my darling Samantha, her skin shimmering with a thin layer of aloe. The stage lights beam down on her, and she smiles and waves. My perfect queen.

She strides down the stage to meet me at the podium, where we exchange a quick embrace. She smells sweet like desert rain, and her muscles feel as tight as a gymnast's. I whisper in her ear,

"They're yours, my love," and hand her the PA mic.

"Hello, my precious children," she says. Her voice already sounds much better than it did post-operation—more warm and natural. "We are gathered here today in celebration of a new age for the chosen essentials, a new way of life for every one of *you*. I know that you are weary from your journey here, and perhaps you still feel some discomfort from your purification process."

She smiles sympathetically, and her tone becomes sweet and soothing. "True change is always painful at first. Believe me when I tell you that I know firsthand. Like you, I have also been reborn."

Her tone turns firm, resolute. "Like you, I've been shown the way to a new life. I used to be weak and afraid, but look at me now. I'm stronger, smarter, faster than I've ever been, and it's all thanks to Jim. All of you will evolve, too, thanks to him. Tell me, are you grateful?"

"YES MOTHER!" the essentials respond. "WE ARE GRATEFUL!"

"Yes, of course you are. A strong leader like Jim is a necessity for our survival. We are blessed to have his wise guidance! So I must remind you of the ground rules. The first and foremost rule is that you must always obey your leader, Jim—your Father. What's the first rule?"

"WE MUST ALWAYS OBEY OUR LEADER, JIM, OUR FATHER! WE MUST ALWAYS OBEY OUR LEADER, JIM, OUR FATHER!" the essentials repeat.

I'm blown away. Samantha is a fucking natural. She has so much swagger, so much charisma—complete fucking dominance over my flock—and she's just getting started.

Samantha commands, "Silence!"

They do as she bids.

"Very good," she says. "Now—"

One gentleman in the first row stands, his hand raised. "I ... I have a question, Samantha ... ma'am ... erm ... Mother ..."

Samantha stares down at him, her eyelids twitching at the interruption. "Patrick P. Livingston, is it not?"

Patrick stutters, "Ye-yes. Sorry, I just arrived, and I was wondering ..."

I glare down at the sniveling fuck. I notice that he's holding a notepad and pen in his hand. What is this guy, the fucking press? Who let him keep such personal items?

"... what do you mean by purification process?" he finishes.

19. ANY MINUTE NOW

My eyelids burst open in a panic. I'm dripping with sweat, lying on my back on a seat in Miss Daisy. Outside, a swollen moon casts its cool light down upon a foreign landscape, a high desert vista scattered with scrabbly shrubs.

I'd been dreaming ... about what? Something that terrified me beyond reason, but I can't remember what.

I sit up and scan the bus. Across the aisle is Carter, and on the seat behind him is Crutch. They're both curled up in the fetal position, sawing logs. Chuck's head sways above the captain's seat, and I see his fingers tapping the steering wheel as if he's listening to a pleasant tune in his head.

I turn around and see Sunshine lying on the floor, propped up on her elbows and writing in a notebook. Behind her is Crutch's electronic monstrosity, a rat's nest of cables connecting towers to dozens of peripherals. She looks up. "Hey, you're awake," she stage-whispers.

I nod. Keeping quiet so I don't disturb Carter and Crutch, I move down the aisle and sit across from her. "Where are we?" I ask.

"We crossed into northern Nevada from Oregon a little while ago."

It hits me—this must be the farthest I've ever been from Bellingham. What am I saying? I've never even left my home state before.

"I was starting to wonder if you were still alive," Sunshine continues. "I'm glad you're up. I wanted to ask you something."

"What's on your mind?"

She pulls herself off her stomach to a cross-legged sitting position that mirrors mine. "The video. The clip of your mother, Max. How can she be alive? I *killed* her; she's been buried. Are you positive it was her in that video?"

The memory of the video Crutch showed us in the trailer crashes down on me. Jim. My mother.

"I'm not one hundred percent certain," I admit.

"Why not?"

"Well ... her voice. It's throwing me off."

"Huh? What about it?"

"It didn't sound anything like her. She sounded weird ... and what's been stirring around in my head is ... okay, bear with me—this might sound crazy ... but she sounded like *Samantha*."

"Samantha? Who's that?"

"Right—you wouldn't know. Um, so let's see ... you remember my old, beat-up Suburban, the one I called the Beast? When I went to work for J & J Funeral, Jim seized my Beast and modified her with a super high-tech AI system. It was all voice-activated, so you could ask it questions and it would respond with the answers."

"Like an Alexa?"

"Kinda, but way creepier, and way more sophisticated. This AI seemed to know everything about everyone. Her name was Samantha." I sigh. "Like I said, I feel crazy. But I swear, it wasn't my mother's voice, even though that woman looked just like her. It was that AI Samantha's."

"Maybe it's just a bad recording? Maybe the sound quality made her sound robotic?" Sunshine sounds hopeful, and I realize what my mother being alive would mean to her—to all the guilt she's been carrying.

Trust me, I want to believe it too, even if she's joined up with Jim for some reason. Because as horrible as that would be, at least she'd still be alive.

With a jolt, the bus dips, then levels out.

"Sorry!" Chuck calls out. "The potholes are like craters out here."

"It's okay, Uncle Chuck," Sunshine responds. "You doing alright? You've been driving all day and night."

"I'm good! Don't worry about me."

"Chuck seems to be holding up just fine," I say to Sunshine. "Didn't he say we were going to stop at a clinic? Did I sleep through it?"

Sunshine sighs. "He keeps saying—

"We're close, any minute now!" Chuck calls out.

"Yeah, right," Sunshine mutters. "It's been *any minute now* for ten hours!"

20. The house of fucking Jim

Sonofabitch. This Patrick asshole somehow slipped through our fingers without getting checked in and chipped.

Samantha stares at the nervous punk in the front row implacably from the stage, not saying a word. The tension builds, reminding me of a classic Western movie stare-down. I could intervene, but I want to see how Samantha handles this.

Patrick fidgets with his pen, and his notepad shakes like a leaf blowing in the wind. The auditorium is quiet, so quiet that you could hear a pen drop. And in fact, that's what happens next. Patrick's pen slips from his hand and strikes the wooden floor. It bounces, spinning in the air, but before it can hit the ground a second time,

Samantha is somehow in front of Patrick with his pen clenched in her hand.

The entire first row gasps. Fuck, it's the whole damn row—they all seem to be thinking without permission. I can imagine their panicked thoughts: *How did she move so quickly? What is she going to do with Patrick?*

Samantha leans toward Patrick and says, "I said, *silence*," then stuffs the pen inside his breast pocket. Patrick's petrified, frozen in place with his eyes bugged out. He manages a nod. She turns, then leaps back onstage and strolls toward the podium, swaying her hips like a runway model— hot damn, I love how she struts!

She says into the PA mic, "Now, repeat after me. I will live in harmony. I will be free. I will follow Jim eternally. Repeat after me! I will live in harmony ..."

The entire auditorium chants, "I will live in harmony. will be free. I will follow Jim eternally!"

Meanwhile, I page Doc. "Doc! Code Red! We have a problem—meet me backstage this instant!"

"Code Red, Jim? The Feds are here?"

"No, goddamnit, that's Code Blue! Code Red!"

"There's been a breach?"

"For fuck's sake, Doc, yes! Now, get your ass over here!" I swear, I've had it with that old geezer.

I drink in a final sight of Samantha before leaving her onstage by her lonesome. She has the auditorium spellbound, under her total control. Samantha, my beauty, you were fucking born for this!

I slip past the velvet curtains and into the dim backstage area where a short set of steps descends to a hallway. Doc appears from around a corner, panting from running. His once-white medical coat is crusted with dried blood.

"Doc, what's going on with these fucks in the auditorium?"

"What do you mean, Jim?"

"The entire front row is acting like they're not chipped!"

"Oh no. Err—I think I know what happened, and maybe, uh, this miscalculation is as simple as needing a—yes! The bioware might need an update, so—Samantha! Yes, she could override them and upload a patch and we can—" He's stumbling over his words, spitting them out so quickly that his face is turning red.

"Goddamnit, Doc, settle down. You're going to give yourself a heart attack! Take a breath and answer one question straight, in fucking English. How many essentials were chipped?"

"Umm ..."

"Were you not keeping track? What's the count?"

"One second, Jim. I have it all right here in my records!" Doc pulls out a spiral pad and flips through his notes. "We chipped 5,007 essentials, sir. We used up all the chips we have."

"Okay, hold that thought, Doc." I activate my lav mic. "Samantha, baby, can you hear me?"

After a moment, she replies, "Yes, Jim."

"Tell me, how many people are in the auditorium right now?"

Two seconds pass, then she tells me, "5,084 people in the auditorium, not counting myself."

"How many are in the front row?"

"Seventy-seven, Jim."

"Thanks, sugar. You're doing great. Keep it up." I address Doc once again. "So, Doc, Samantha tells me that there are 5,084. Sounds like all seventy-seven in the front row are not chipped! Jesus, Doc! You better give me a good reason why this happened, and do it quick before I lose my goddamn temper!"

Doc exhales sharply. "Jim, I believe there were some late arrivals, and you recalled all our chipped aides to the auditorium, so there wasn't anyone to—"

"Are you trying to pin this shit on me, Doc?" I narrow my eyes at his nerve.

"No, no, not at all—"

"Because if I recall correctly, I left *you* in

charge of chipping all the essentials! Under no circumstance can these seventy-seven be permitted to leave the grounds! They've seen and heard too much!"

"Yes, Jim. I agree."

Goddamnit! *They* can't find out about this mishap. "Doc, how are the Holtzes holding up?"

"Last I checked, they're fine. Holtz is recovering nicely."

"Good. Make sure they don't hear about this little hiccup. Got it?"

"Of course. We mustn't trouble Holtz while he's in a delicate state."

Now the question is, do I handle the front row personally, or do I delegate?

"Junior," I bark. "Junior, Jim here. Where are you?"

"Junior here ... I'm—" Electronic static fills my earpiece.

"What was that, Junior? Junior, do you copy?"

Samantha's voice reverberates down the hall: "You will be essential! You will live in harmony! And you! And you! You! All essential! Who wants to live free of worry? Who loves Father? I can't hear you!" The audience goes wild, their roars shaking the walls of the megachurch. She's doing a fantastic job with the neural imprinting, but this racket is making it impossible to think straight.

"Junior! Do you fucking copy!"

All I hear on my earpiece is static. "Shit on a stick," I mutter as I run my fingers through my hair, trying to keep my cool. I'm getting fed up. I can't let the Project Exodus gears gum up to a grinding halt.

"Okay, Doc, this is the plan. We split up. You keep the Holtzes on ice and find Junior, and when you do, you tell no-neck to page me. Let me handle the chipless fucks, and you better hope to hell that nobody leaves this fucking church without a chip in their head. Now, scram!"

This whole thing has become another goddamn shitshow, thanks again to the incompetence of those around me. Doc has made us trip at the finish line and fall flat on our faces. But the race isn't over yet. I need to push forward, and if I must make an entire row of people disappear off the face of this earth, I don't give a shit.

As I head back to the auditorium, I remind myself to keep cool before I set foot onstage. My window of time to imprint the chipped essentials narrows every minute. I can show them no fear, no weakness.

It's time to get with it. Jim, you handsome devil, show these people who's boss. Remind them that they're in the house of fucking Jim—that's me! I'm in control, not them! Fuck yeah, let's get pumped up, Jim! Come on, bring on the explosive energy! Be the loudest, the smartest, the most charming fucking guy in the room, Jim! Stand up straight, Jim! You're the best, Jim! Jim!! JIM!! JIM!!!

That's better.

21. Thumb to his Heart

"Slow down, Chuck!" I scream.

Loose rocks kick up against Miss Daisy's undercarriage, and the suspension squeaks. Chuck's steered us off the highway and onto a dusty one-lane road.

"Uncle Chuck!" Sunshine cries from behind Carter. "I think you need to take a nap!"

"Sweetie, for the six-hundredth time, I'm fine! Besides, I'm the one with the Teamster license. I tell ya, this is nothing. I used to drive across the country just for the heck of it!"

"That was years ago!" Carter grumbles. "I wasn't even born then!"

"Carter's right, you know," Sunshine says. "It's not safe for anyone to be driving for so long, especially someone in your condition."

"I can't do too much about the bumps, gang, but we're almost there."

"Almost where?" Carter asks.

"I told you, to a place that's got both gas and medicine!"

I don't want to get involved in this quarrel. I scoot off my bench seat and head to the back.

Crutch sits there cross-legged, tinkering with some black box. He's partially dismantled its casing and wired a bunch of cables into it that feed into his laptop. That laptop, in turn, is connected to a PC tower working overtime, whirring and humming with activity.

His setup is impressive, but what amazes me more is that he's able to maneuver a micro screwdriver in one hand and pinch screws with the other while the bus shakes like a derailed roller coaster car.

I can hardly keep myself from falling over, so I take a seat on the floor facing Crutch. He's rigged up power from the bus to his electronics, and he's even plugged my phone into a USB port to charge. I have no desire to turn it back on yet, though.

Off in the distance, through the emergency exit glass, I spot a moving train atop a ridge. It's no passenger train—it's hauling military vehicles, hundreds of them, lined up one after another. Where are they headed? What's Crutch doing? Is

Chuck going to be okay? I'm starting to feel like I don't know anything about what's going on.

For a while now, I've been having this haunting feeling that forces are in play outside of my comprehension or control. I can't put my finger on it, but it fills me with a sense of doom. I feel like a character in a dramatic play who's beginning to suspect that the end is already written—and worse, I've forgotten my fucking lines.

Since I woke up at Chuck's, the world has completely shifted; there's a mandatory draft, an all-out war has begun, and now I'm on a school bus heading south to rescue my mother, who somehow seems to be alive and in some unholy alliance with Jim. As the song goes, things aren't like they used to be. What's next? Bring on the aliens; I'm ready.

The one thing that makes sense in this crazy fucking world is the people inside this bus. Beyond these steel walls? Unpredictable insanity. God, maybe it would do me some good to interact and get out of my head.

I turn back to Crutch, who's twisting together strands of copper wire. "Crutch, can I ask you something?"

"Yeah, what is—" Distracted, he drops a wire, and it bounces off the floor like a spring.

I have so many questions. Say, Crutch, how

did you know about that spyware on my phone? What are you doing with all this stuff now? On second thought, though, he seems so focused on his task, whatever it is he's doing. I don't want to disturb the little guy's concentration with questions. "Forget it," I say. "Let me know if you need anything, okay?"

I get to my feet and return to the front. Through the windshield, I see a lit gas station in the middle of nowhere, some fifty yards ahead. It's small, with a few gas pumps next to a convenience store. A colorful neon sign on a pole reads: Bohagande Fuel & RX. It looks nearly abandoned, save for the late '80s Toyota pickup truck parked just outside the store.

Chuck pulls Daisy close to a gas pump and kills the engine and the headlights. He rips the air horn three times and says, "Shouldn't be long."

"Pops, where the hell have you brought us?" Carter gripes. "This place is a ghost town. I thought you said there's a clinic."

The sound of a door chime signals the exit of two men from the store, dressed casually in blue jeans and flannel shirts. They approach us, somehow matching strides even though one is a full head shorter than the other.

"Pops, who are these guys?"

"They're old friends of mine," Chuck says, standing. "With a bit of luck, old Daisy and I will be feeling much better soon, and we'll be on our way."

"With a bit of luck?" Carter asks, throwing his arms in the air. "What's that supposed to mean?"

"Gang, this might not look like it, but these pumps hold the best gas in the region, high-quality octane, and I know Daisy here would appreciate some decent fuel in her belly," Chuck tells us, ignoring his son's question. "You should get something in your bellies, too. Hang tight, and have yourselves a little road snack. I'll be right back."

Chuck shuffles outside. We press our faces to the bus's windows, trying to get a better look at the strangers. They appear to be around Chuck's age, with chestnut skin and tied-back, silver-streaked black hair.

Chuck greets them with some kind of sign language. He jabs his thumb to his heart, then back at us, then back at them. The men smile and respond with their own gestures. The three of them begin to talk. About what, I don't know; I can't read lips.

Chuck lifts his wallet from his back pocket, pulls out a card, and hands it to the shorter of his two friends. The man takes it, then moseys toward the gas pump and begins filling Daisy with diesel. Chuck then lifts his shirt, and the taller man frowns and shakes his head.

I haven't seen the big guy's wound since I

cleaned it, and I can't imagine what it looks like now underneath the gauze. How the hell has Chuck driven this far? He should be dead, or in a deep coma at the very least. Is he some kind of superhuman? I sure thought so when I was a kid, but this kind of endurance screams that he's some kind of freak.

"Old friends?" Carter grumbles. "I've never seen them before in my life."

"Well, Chuck is sure acting like they're buddies, am I right?" I ask.

Carter lets out an agitated sigh. "I don't know, man. Maybe, I guess. Pops won't tell me anything, and you know what? I don't give a shit right now—I'm starving. Hey, are there any of those crackers around?"

"Yeah, I think so. Go ask Crutch."

"Hey, *Crotch*! Why don't you stop fiddling with that shit and tell me where the Ritz and peanut butter is at?"

"Jesus, Carter. You don't have to be such a bully," Sunshine says. "Ask nicely."

"Nah, I just like reminding the kid who's in charge every once in a while." Carter leans in and whispers, "Brother, between you and me, I still don't trust that sneaky ginger."

"What's got you in such a shitty mood?" Sunshine asks.

"Oh, I don't know, cuz. Maybe it's because

we're in the middle of nowhere hiding from the fucking *draft*, Pops won't go to a real hospital, and Max's mom's been kidnapped by a *psycho*?"

"I get it! We're all in the same boat here. Why don't you relax? There's no reason to be picking on somebody just because the world's gone crazy."

"Don't tell me to relax! My nerves are fried, and I can't stop obsessing about how Pops could croak at any minute! And if he goes, well, I don't know what I'll do, so excuse me for being in a shitty mood! I've had about enough of this—"

"Here," Crutch says, wandering up to the front of the bus, a sleeve of Ritz crackers and an open jar of peanut butter in his hands.

Carter rips the sleeve open, shoves a handful of Ritz into the Jif, then jams the crackers into his mouth. He chews like a starved dog, gulps, belches, then says, "Sorry, cuz. My blood sugar levels were low."

"How about saying that to him?" Sunshine jerks her head toward Crutch. "He suffered just as much as any of us—much more. We're all the family he's got left, so treat him like it!"

Spitting crumbs, Carter says, "Fine. Sorry, little guy. I was being a dick."

Crutch shrugs and scurries back to the rear of the bus, where he settles himself once again on his rat's nest of cables and beeping electronics.

"Hey! No hard feelings, Crutch?" Carter calls down to him.

"Nope," Crutch says, not looking up. The kid never seems the least bit concerned about Carter's insults; he lets them bounce off him like he's made of rubber. I wish I were so resilient.

"See," Carter says, spraying cracker bits everywhere. "We're all cordial. Just a bunch of friendly old chums on this stinkin' bus."

Miss Daisy's doors slide open. Chuck climbs in and drops into the captain's chair, looking as if the past day's exertions have caught up to him at last. He's no superhuman now—he looks old, weary, and with one foot in the grave. I glance outside, and Chuck's buddies are nowhere in sight. What now?

Carter says, "Pops, as soon as the tanks are full, you need to drive to the closest hospital."

"Don't worry about me, son," Chuck replies, but his voice lacks conviction.

I blurt out, "Come on, Chuck! Cut the fucking bullshit!"

Everyone's attention snaps to me, and I continue. "Explain to all of us how in the holy hell you are going to get through this! How will you survive another day, Chuck? Carter is right, we need to get you to a fucking hospital!"

Quiet descends on the bus. I realize I've never spoken to him like this before. Chuck adjusts the rearview mirror, and our gazes lock through the reflection. For a blip, his eyes, usually full of certainty, now flicker with something else—desperation and sadness. Does the big guy know that he's close to his end?

Chuck grins, and the pained look on his face melts away as if it were never there. "I'll be fine, because my old friends here," he says, his voice steady, "they're taking me to their healer."

22. LOOK AT ME NOW

"Samantha, baby, get this crowd roaring for me." It's time for yours truly to pick up where he left off.

"Yes, Jim," Samantha replies. Her voice pierces through the PA system, "Let's hear it for our great leader!"

The audience chants, "Father! Father!"

I stride back onto the stage, flashing my stupendous CEO grin and waving to the essentials, who erupt in thunderous cheer.

Goddamn, Samantha, you have been doing such a stand-up job cramming them with my teachings, reminding them who's in charge and who to trust. Her lessons have paid off; the deafening ovation rattles the lights above the stage. I encourage them to yell even louder, raising my hands above my head. I'm like a Hoover, sucking the energy out of them. God, I love me.

"Father, Father!" they scream.

I stretch my hands toward the vaulted ceiling, projecting triumph and confidence.

"Father! Father!"

I want nothing else but to savor this moment forever, to bottle it up and store it for safekeeping. Right here, right now, there's no one in this world more important than, well, me!

"FATHER! FATHER!"

I sweep my gaze across the congregation with joy. Alas, I'm bluntly reminded of my task at hand by the sight of the front row. Their bewildered faces expose the truth of their non-chipped brains. I need them gone fast, and without disturbing my true essentials.

I pluck the PA mic from Samantha's hand and say into it, "Sounds like we're having a great time. How are you all feeling?"

The auditorium choruses, "Fan-fuckin'-tastic, Father!"

I've never been able to communicate with them like this before. The Bellingham essentials would follow commands through a manual controller—attack, stand guard, obey—but never with this level of enthusiasm or responsiveness. They're growing into something greater than I ever imagined. Sheer emotion swells deep within me.

Come on Jim, keep it together! Focus, you beautiful bastard!

I stab my finger at the first row in the auditorium. "My essentials, congratulations! The time has come for your purification! Yes! All of you in the front row, don't be shy. Please join me onstage, and I will personally prepare you for paradise!"

The essentials in the front stand and trickle toward me. I count them as they climb onstage ... seventy-five ... seventy-six ... seventy-seven!

As I watch them line up before me, a wave of nausea courses through my body. I despise them. These fucking asswipes move when they shouldn't, laugh at all the wrong times; they babble, they fart, they cough. They're disgusting, and one hundred percent non-chipped. Even if they begged on their knees to come along on the ride to my kingdom, I wouldn't let them. If you're not chipped, then you're nothing but an undeserving sassy bitch.

I never stop smiling. If they get spooked, they might run off like the cowardly sheep they are. They'd flee and tell the world about us, about me and Samantha and my essentials, and that's a no-no.

"My children!" I shout. "Please give your

soon-to-be-purified brothers and sisters a warm round of applause!"

My true essentials cheer. The assfucks on the stage bow and wave, grinning and basking in the attention. *True* essentials would never respond in such a way—not unless I commanded it.

I contemplate the many ways I could delete them from existence. I've been dealing with death for over two decades. I've scraped bodies off highway pavement, removed severed limbs from car wrecks, and pulled bloated floaters from rivers and lakes. I've buried corpses destroyed by bullets, knives, diseases, and poisons. You fucking name it and I've seen it, and baby, you bet your ass I moved it! Maybe one day, I'll write a book about it.

As the mortuary director at J & J Funeral, I was the one responsible for cleaning up the shit after the action. This time, I get to be the one holding the smoking gun! But I'd prefer not to make a mess; this purge must be quick and quiet, and I have just the thing. I will wash away their sins!

"This way, my essentials," I say to the soon-to-be-purged bastards. I stride confidently behind the curtains. "Single file now, and wait for me in the hallway," I tell them, waving them past me. One by one, they obey. I glance at their necks as they pass. As expected, there's no evidence of a single stitch.

I whisper into my lav mic, "My queen, begin the next phase of Project Exodus."

"Your wish is my command."

God, I love her.

I pluck a coiled extension cord from a tech rack and tuck it under my blazer, then head down to join the seventy-seven fuckwads. They're staring at me, shoulder-to-shoulder in the hallway.

"Coming through!" I shout. After I elbow aside the first few in my way, the rest shuffle aside. Once I've pushed through them all, I call out, "This way, my essentials, and do not make a sound."

As I turn and begin walking, I can hear whispers from behind me: *Where is he taking us?—How would I know?—Shut up, stupid, Jim or Father, whoever he is, he said, no talking—I have to pee!*

These pathetic morons can't go for one second without babbling whatever stray thought passes through their minds. Christ! I can't wait until this part is over. I crane my neck around to flash them a reassuring smile. "I understand you might be tired, as I know it's been a tremendous day, but I will not say this again. Please keep your comments to yourself until we've reached our destination."

I lead them through an archway into the church's Fellowship Hall, pass through it into a prayer garden, then beyond that, through a maze of winding passages.

I'm rather glad that our destination is at the other end of the main building, as it gives me more of a chance to soak in the splendor of this heavenly sanctuary. The Holtzes snowbird a couple months a year in Arizona, and being devout Baptists (so they say), the Holtzes would never miss a weekly service. And they can't go to just any raggedy-ass cowtown chapel for service, no, not the Holtzes. So, the filthy rich family dropped a serious chunk of cha-ching to build this grand cathedral. Half its space is devoted to the auditorium alone.

One might wonder, why make an auditorium so grandiose? Image, baby. When a pastor speaks, it's necessary to have an amplified, clear voice backed up with visual projection. The words flowing from the pastor's lips must be loud and crisp, the images crystal clear. If there's the slightest crackle from a cheap PA, it's over. How could you convince a crowd that you speak for God if your voice is muffled or full of static? The congregation must believe that God Himself is speaking through you—there can be no doubt.

It's easy to do if you believe in the product you're selling, and I sure-as-fuck do. Like a pastor's, my product is irresistible—carefree life inside a blissful garden. A fertile Eden where my essentials can live without stress, without hunger, with purpose!

Still, as perfect as our paradise will be, it's a damn shame that we must leave this church tonight. I'm starting to dig this place. If the FBI didn't have a hard-on for yours truly, I'd consider settling down here. But I must keep moving—that's the trick of survival. That's how I've made it this far.

But I'm no sewer rat merely trying to survive. I'm meant for a grander destiny. I knew it the moment I first met Holtz. It wasn't just luck that I crossed paths with a man of such wealth and power, setting me up to achieve my true potential.

I stop before a large steel door that reads *BAPTISM*, each italicized letter the size of my fist. I turn to face my followers. They're quiet as they wait for my direction, but I must act before this flock becomes restless. Who knows?—at any moment, these bastards could make a run for it.

But for now, they're placid and docile, and why wouldn't they be? They chose to be here. All their lives, they have been waiting for a be-all, end-all pill to save them from suffering. They want the easy fix, someone to provide them with purpose. And I *will* provide purpose, just not for these fucks!

I clear my throat and say, "Welcome, my essentials, to the purification chamber! Before we begin, there are some ground rules. The space beyond this door is sacred, so you must remain quiet. Cleanliness is key, so everyone must remove their shoes and socks before entering. You can leave them here in the hallway. Now—"

"Excuse me, Jim, umm ... Father. One question, please," an awkward-looking bastard with oily skin and hair like a mop interrupts me. "You said shoes *and* socks off?"

"Yes! Did I stutter? No shoes, no socks! All must come off unless you want to be cast out with your tail between your legs. Is that what you want?"

He shakes his head and mutters, "No."

"I thought not. Now, does anyone else have a problem following the ground rules? Anyone? Speak now, or forever hold your peace!"

Not a peep. I shine another irresistible CEO smirk. "Fan-fuckin'-tastic. One at a time now."

I unlock the *BAPTISM* door, revealing a spiral staircase that descends to a lower level. I double-check my headcount as they move past me. *One, two, three* ... one by one, the sheep shuffle quietly down the stairs.

Thud ... thud ... *thirty-three, thirty-four.* The sounds of their naked feet slapping against the cool concrete steps echo up to me.

Thud ... thud ... *fifty ... fifty-one* ... A pleasurable shiver runs up my spine as I savor how even these non-chipped bastards obey me—it's almost as sweet as the complete control I exert over the others. But it's not enough to save them from their fate.

Thud ... thud ... *Seventy-six ... seventy-fucking-seven.*

I close the door. The lock snaps into place with a metallic bite, sharp and unforgiving.

23. Sit in stifling silence

We wait as diesel pours into Miss Daisy's twin tanks. Nobody seems to be in a talkative mood. We're all spent and tired of bickering, even Carter. I wish that there was a radio we could turn on to hear some music; hell, I'd even listen to country or jazz at this point. Lacking entertainment, I watch as miniature dust tornadoes wander haphazardly across the neon-lit cracked pavement, then collapse, again and again.

The convenience store's door chimes and the two men are once again approaching the bus. "Here we go," Chuck says under his breath.

A gust of wind makes its way inside as the men climb aboard. "Big Chuck," says the taller one, "She's ready for you, and you alone."

Chuck tries to stand but stumbles, his legs

shaking. His friends grab him as he slumps to the floor.

Carter stands and shouts, "No way! I'm coming with him!"

The shorter man shakes his head. "Stay, boy. He must face his fate alone."

Carter turns bright red in the face and starts spluttering and cursing.

"Listen to them, son!" Chuck says. The two men hoist him by his shoulders and feet and lug him outside. They transport the big guy toward the convenience store like he weighs nothing.

Framed in the store entrance is a tiny, ancient woman with long, snow-colored braids. She steps aside as the two men carry Chuck into the store. The door slides shut. A hand flips over the OPEN sign hanging on the door so that it reads CLOSED.

Carter races off the bus toward the store. Sunshine and I watch from inside as he yanks at the door. It doesn't seem to budge an inch, so he pounds on it with his fists and feet, shouting, "Let me in! What are you doing with my Pops? Open this damn door—fuuuck!"

"Carter, come on," Sunshine calls to him. "Your Pops said he'll be alright."

Carter returns to the bus, huffing and puffing as he struggles to catch his breath. I toss him a water bottle, and he downs it in one gulp.

"Are you guys seriously okay with this?" Carter growls at us. "What kind of medical equipment do they have back there? A nacho cheese dispenser? A Slurpee machine?"

"I wouldn't worry about it too much, cuz," Sunshine says. "Call it a hunch, but something tells me that Chuck will be okay."

"A hunch, huh?" Carter says, throwing his empty water bottle to the floor in disgust. "Max, what about you? You're awfully quiet. How do you feel about this?"

"I'm with Sunshine," I say. "Let's just wait it out and see."

"Yeah, wait it out. You fucking guys. Jesus." Carter flings himself into the captain's chair and turns his back to us. We sit in stifling silence, Sunshine and I taking up the first two bench beats across from each other. The tension is thick enough to choke a horse. All I can hear is Crutch's endless tinkering in the rear. Each clink, tap, and whack of his tools is starting to grate on my nerves. Where is Chuck? What's taking them so long?

"AAAAAHAAHHHAHAHA!"

An unearthly scream echoes across the gas station, throbbing with a depth of pain I've never heard before. "Pops!" Carter screams. He dashes off the bus toward the convenience store once again, this time with Sunshine and me right at his heels.

Just as Carter reaches the door, it slides open, and the men carry Chuck out and toward the bus. "Pops! Can you hear me? What have you done with him?" Carter cries, walking in unison with them, but Chuck appears to be out cold—or worse.

A sharp whistle pulls my attention back toward the convenience store. In its doorway, the ancient woman from earlier is waving at us.

I nudge Sunshine. "Hey, look, I think she wants to talk to us."

The woman smiles, her eyes becoming slits of happiness as we walk toward her. She points toward Chuck, then puts her palms together and lays them against the side of her cheek, tilting her head. She closes her eyes and starts to breathe heavily, as if sleeping.

Sunshine turns toward me. "She's telling us that Chuck needs to sleep," she says.

The woman's eyes pop open, and she beams merrily at Sunshine. She reaches into her dress and pulls out a leather pouch dangling from a looped cord, no larger than a child's sack for marbles. She beckons for Sunshine to come closer and lower her head. Rising on her tip-toes, she places the pouch around Sunshine's neck, then whispers into her ear.

"What did she just say, Sunshine?" I ask. "What's in that?"

"Medicine," Sunshine answers, holding up

the pouch. "She says it'll teach Chuck's body how to heal. I think that's what she said, anyway." She loosens its drawstrings and peers inside it.

The ancient woman taps Sunshine to get her attention and pats her own lips.

"He's supposed to take the medicine by mouth," Sunshine translates, mirroring the woman's gestures.

The woman nods vigorously, then turns to me and thumps the tips of her fingers against my sternum, hard. Ouch! "What do you want?" I ask.

She rubs her thumb and forefinger together quickly, then flattens her palm out toward me.

"Payment?"

The ancient woman nods. I draw my wallet from the ass pocket of my jeans, pull out my emergency Benjamin, and place the bill in her hand. She grins, winks at me, then heads back into the convenience store. Chuck's two friends exit the bus and follow her inside. "Give Chuck our best," one of the men says as they pass us.

"AAAHHHAHAHHHHA!"

Another terrible moan from the bus makes me wince, but hey, at least that sound means the big guy is alive. Sunshine and I hightail it toward Miss Daisy, and once inside, I see Chuck lying in the middle of the aisle with his head pointed toward the back, kicking and screaming. Carter and

Crutch are trying to hold him down from the other side.

"Max, help!" Carter cries. "Pops is freaking out!"

I rush over and do my best to pin his legs, but Chuck keeps thrashing.

"Uncle Chuck, stop! You're making it worse!" Sunshine cries, her voice shaking. "Relax, just take it easy. Let me see what's going on."

Chuck stops screaming and relaxes, giving Sunshine a chance to lift his shirt. I wish she hadn't. Covering the infection site now are tiny crawling creatures—hundreds of them, white and writhing over his flesh. It's an image I instantly wish I could scrub from my eyeballs.

"Holy shit, are those fucking maggots on my Pops?!" Carter yells.

"Yeah, those are maggots alright," Sunshine says. "But it's okay! I learned about this in my naturopathy school. They're eating away the infected tissue. It hurts, but it should help."

"*AAAHAHAHAHAAAAH!*"

Chuck lets out another agonized wail. Carter and Crutch hang onto his arms, using their weight to keep him from tearing at his stomach. "How is this *helping*, cuz?" Carter shouts.

"What about that pouch?" I ask Sunshine. "Whatever's in it is supposed to help him heal, right?"

She nods and digs into the leather pouch around her neck. Pulling out a handful of opalescent pink powder, she hurls a handful into Chuck's gaping mouth. The reaction is immediate. Chuck's body seizes with a flurry of violent shivers, then his muscles relax and his eyes close.

Carter presses his fingers desperately against his father's throat and says, "He's breathing, but—cuz, what the flippin' fuck was in that pouch?"

"Medicine," Sunshine says, shrugging.

24. WHAT GOES UP MUST COME DOWN

My mother passed away following my premature birth, and my father was a violent man who drank himself to an early grave before my tenth year on Earth. The state snatched me up and drop-kicked me into the foster care system. It was there that I began to rebel.

I set fires inside trash cans and got into dozens of physical and verbal altercations. I disrespected the foster parents and manipulated my social workers. They labeled me a bad seed. Instead of trying to medicate the root of my problems, the state stepped in and removed me like a rotten tooth, ripping me out of each foster home and implanting me into another—thirteen times before I turned eighteen.

One foster parent suggested that I should

pray. "Pray, Jim, pray to the almighty God and ask Him to save your soul," he would say.

Pray to a God? Why would a God let an innocent child's mother die, leaving the defenseless thing with an abusive drunk of a father? God must have a sick and twisted sense of humor. And maybe I do too, but hey, I'm made in His image, right?

I laugh at the idea that there's a know-all puppet master in the clouds, watching and judging from above. I imagine Him using His powers to spy on people taking showers, shitting, pissing, jacking off—ha! He sounds like a perverted control freak, if you ask me. God loves us? No, God despises humanity.

There was a time in my life when I thought differently about the Almighty. I was a young man only a few years out of the foster care system when I met Jane. She seemed like a beautiful angel. I recall thinking that maybe God sent Jane to me as consolation, to make amends for my horrible childhood. Perhaps God wasn't so bad after all.

I doted on Jane, and we were married the next year. She said she loved me, and I said I loved her. We were going to raise a family together. Life was wonderful. For the first time in my life, my heart was full. That was, until she ripped it out of my chest and stomped it to fucking pieces. She terminated our child, our family, and our future. "There is evil in you, Jim," she said, "and I will not raise a family with the Devil in disguise. I'm leaving you tonight!"

Bitch! Whore! How could you? I screamed, and yes, I hit her like my drunk father used to hit me, and yes, she hit me back, and so of course I retaliated, and she bled, she called the police, and yes, I was arrested, and sent to jail, and yes, my anger grew exponentially. The bad seed inside me grew into a poisonous nettle that choked me from the inside, and I soon realized that like God, I too despised all of humanity!

I wanted nothing to do with the people who walked around with their perfect lives, their God-saved souls, their well-behaved families, their well-kept lawns. Their puppies and baby showers and anniversary dinners and all that horseshit.

After I served my sentence, I was pissed off and lost, to say the least. I was a ticking time bomb, just waiting for the next excuse to lash out in an incoherent rage, a rage so strong it would hurl me once more behind iron bars. That was, until while slinging drinks at a banquet, I met a rich and powerful man.

Holtz was his name and he saw the potential in me, behind the burning in my eyes. It was he, Holtz, who sent me to J & J. It was there that I learned how to cope with my distaste for humankind by burying the dead. I worked my way up from hauling bodies to mortuary director, and it was then that I first tasted authority and the power it brings.

And yes, I was happy, and yes, I loved my job. But to tell you the truth, I'm glad that gig didn't work out in the end, because now I believe I have found my true calling—to be on stage with a mic in my hand, preaching to my adoring masses!

Now, as I walk down this staircase toward the seventy-seven souls waiting for yours truly, I can't stop thinking *what if?*

What if I'd stumbled upon this heavenly place at an earlier age—would my life have turned out differently? How many people would I have under my control by now if, instead of marrying Jane at age twenty-four, I had realized my calling?

But then again, I shouldn't wonder about the what-ifs. It's better late than never. I can't complain—look how I've turned out. I'm transforming people into a strengthened species, all for a higher purpose! I've gathered thousands of essential soldiers who will follow me faithfully. Yes, me, my smile, my charm, my sharp wit! I have become a God, a father to thousands. Suck on that, Jane!

As I step from the bottom stair into the lower chamber, I see them, all seventy-seven, gathered around a white marble baptismal pool. Like everything else in the Church of the Holy Desert, this puppy is mega-sized. I've never had one myself, a baptism, but from what I understand, the process comprises a series of prayers and a symbolic water submersion intended to purify one's body, mind, and spirit—a kind of metaphorical metamorphosis, if you will.

I can't be interrupted during what comes next. I pluck out my earpiece and stuff it into a pocket before I begin to speak.

"My precious essentials, today you shall cross over to a new chapter of your existence. I shall wash away your fears and set you on the path toward enlightenment. Now, you must climb into the holy water and form one large circle."

Sounds of discontent fester throughout the group, but I put a stop to it by raising my hands and shouting, "People! I assure you that the water won't bite. This is a cleansing, a necessary step to begin your journey toward everlasting life. Must I remind you what's happening outside these walls? Hell has broken loose, and this is your opportunity to get to my heaven on Earth! Now, who's ready to be saved?"

Without further protest, one by one, they step into the holy water and stand tightly together, packing themselves into one large seventy-seven-person circle.

"This water is freezing!" yells some guy at the far end of the pool. "I can't feel my toes!"

These fucking babies are pissing me off. "You'll get used to the temperature soon enough," I tell him.

I'm no physics expert, but I recall a few things from ninth-grade science class. One is that electricity takes the path of least resistance, spreading out and moving at incredible speeds as it tries to create a full circuit. Yes, and if memory serves, salt water, like the kind inside this baptismal pool, is a perfect conductor of electrical current. The sodium and chloride ions from the salts are charged particles that let electricity flow through the water effortlessly. Damn, I love science.

I tell them, "Listen closely. I want each of you to reach out and grab hold of a neighbor's hands."

They obey me, joining together by their hands.

"Fan-fuckin'-tastic," I say. "My children, close your eyes and visualize the rolling hills of the paradise I've shown you."

They close their eyes.

On a marble table behind me is an unplugged Sony boombox, equipped with a CD player, two tape decks, plus an AM/FM radio. I jam one end of the extension cord I swiped earlier into a wall outlet, then connect the boombox to it. The boombox lights up and the

CD player's cover opens. Calligraphic text on the disc inside reads: *Pavarotti - Ave Maria.* Good enough for me. I press PLAY, and the music begins.

A gentle instrumental introduction of strings and woodwinds creates a serene atmosphere. I walk toward the baptismal pool, holding the boombox high above my head, just like John Cusack's character in that shitty flick *Say Anything.*

"Do you remember why you're here?" I ask.

"Yes," they answer in unison, their eyes shut, knee-deep in salt water.

"You sought me out because you were lost in an uncaring world, and you are now found! Tell me, my children, do you wish to become one of the chosen?"

"Yes!" the seventy-seven cry out.

"Good! Now repeat after me, I am essential! Father, set us free!"

The baptismal chamber echoes with their words, "I am essential! Father, set us free!"

"AGAIN!"

"I am essential! Father, set us free!"

I turn the volume up on the stereo to the max. The tremendous and tender voice of a man begins to sing about I-don't-know-what; it's Latin, which makes it feel powerful. "Louder!" I yell. "I can't hear you!"

"I AM ESSENTIAL! FATHER, SET US FREE!"

"Yes! I, Jim! I will set you free!"

I toss the boombox into the air above the pool.

"I AM ESSENTIAL! FATHER, SET US FREE!"

The boombox begins to fall, because what I also recall from physics class is that what goes up must come down.

"I AM ESSENTIAL! FATHER, SET US FREE!"

My heart flutters with joy as the electrified boombox twists and turns, descending toward the holy water, with the flutes playing, the strings strumming, the man singing, and the seventy-seven chanting—until—kerplunk!—*ZAAAAP!*

They scream for half a second before the electricity fries their voice boxes. And oh boy, that beautiful unified scream shoots through my body like the energy coursing through theirs. Their pain is my pleasure.

They flail and twitch, and some try to escape the pool, but their muscles seize up and their hearts stop. Like bowling pins, they topple over into the water. Smoke rises as their bodies sizzle like sausages over a fire, their insides cooking to a crisp. And soon, too soon if you ask me, it's over.

I leave them there for the time being and hustle back toward the auditorium, but I'm cut short en route to my destination. "Jim!" Doc says, running toward me. For an old fart, he has some serious lungs. He skids to a stop four inches from my chest.

"Jesus, Doc. Will you ease up? You're killing my buzz. What the hell is it now?"

"The Holtzes called for an emergency meeting. They want you and me in their suite at once!"

"Regarding what? Is Holtz okay?"

"He's as well as can be expected."

"Well, what is it then?"

"I don't know, but I suppose we're going to find out."

25. Empty, endless highway

Chuck's out cold in the aisle, snoring like a buzz saw. He could definitely use the rest. Unfortunately for the rest of us, our map to Snake Bend is in his head, and the moon is growing fuller by the minute. At least Miss Daisy's tanks are full.

"My phone's still not getting a signal," Sunshine says, her voice tight. "What about you guys?"

"I don't have my freakin' phone," Carter snaps. "Left it at the house, remember?"

"Crutch, what are you doing with that?" I ask.

The kid's hunched over his laptop, my cell phone in hand. Without looking up, he mutters, "All the major U.S. networks are down, but I rigged up a temporary satellite connection and downloaded a bunch of eSIMs to your phone.

Found one that gets a decent signal, and now my laptop can hotspot off it."

"Why didn't you tell us, you little twerp?" Carter growls.

Crutch shrugs. "Just got it working. Come check it out."

Sunshine and I climb over a bus seat to get past the sleeping big guy. We all drop to the floor beside Crutch.

"I can map us to Snake Bend using back roads, just like Chuck would," Crutch says, fingers flying over the laptop keyboard. The screen lights up with a digital map. "I've downloaded a step-by-step map. And right now, we're outside Battle Mountain, Nevada. It says here that we should hit the NV-376, which is—"

Carter cuts in, "Hold up, Nevada? That's next to Arizona, right? So we're maybe a few hours away?"

"Well, we're halfway to Snake Bend, so more like a half day away."

Carter's shoulders slump. "Fuck man, I can't spend another second on this stinkin' bus. Who's gonna drive, then? Anyone know how to drive stick other than my Pops?"

"Sorry, not me," Sunshine says. "Anyway, I should keep an eye on Uncle Chuck's condition. Max?"

"Nope."

"What about you, carrot top?" Carter asks. "It's your dad's stupid bus."

"I can't reach the pedals," Crutch says.

"Well, *someone* needs to fucking move this hunk of tin," Carter snaps.

Just how hard can it be to drive stick? Millions of people do it.

"Listen, everyone. I've got a plan," I tell them, rising to my feet. "Sunshine, you're right. You need to stay with Chuck. Make sure he's breathing—and get some rest yourself. You'll need it."

She looks up at me and nods. "Got it, Max. I just want to help get your mom back."

"You and me both." I turn to Crutch, who's still glued to his laptop. "Crutch, can you download videos?"

"For now, yeah. What do you need?"

"A how-to on driving a stick."

"On it."

"Good. And you're gonna be my co-pilot. Keep track of exactly where we are, and I mean *exactly*."

"What about me? What am I, chopped liver?" Carter asks. "What's my job?"

"Carter, you're on lookout duty. We'll need extra eyes on the road. Spot anything—cars, people, trouble. You're on it."

"Lookout, huh? Wait, I've got just the thing!"

Carter exclaims, jumping up. He scurries toward the shelving in the rear, then returns with a pair of familiar high-tech binoculars in his hands. "I grabbed these from the Jeep. But what about you?" he asks me. "You're gonna drive?"

"You're damn right I'm driving. Let's move."

I head to the front of the bus, my boots echoing on the metal floor. Dropping into the captain's seat, I grip the wheel. Confidence felt easy a second ago, but now, staring at the controls, doubt creeps in. This isn't just big—it's *huge*. The wheel is massive, and the pedals are spread far apart. The Beast felt like a tank, but this? This is a spaceship.

Alright, Max. One step at a time.

Keys—they're in the ignition. Good. I twist them, and the dashboard comes alive. Lights flicker and needles twitch, and the low hum of the battery power settles in.

I glance back. "Crutch, how's that video coming?"

"Got it!" he says, trotting toward me with his laptop. He spins its screen around to play me a video. The calm voice of a driving instructor guides me over the laptop speakers: "Start by finding the clutch—it's on the far left, see, there? The engine won't start unless you press it down."

Right, the clutch. I've heard of that before. My left foot finds the pedal and pushes. I twist the key again, and the engine roars to life. I square my shoulders and grip the wheel tightly. "Alright, now what?"

"Jam the gear shifter into first," Crutch says, showing me the next part of the video. I grab the shifter and shove it up and to the left. The driving instructor's voice tells me, "Ease off the clutch as you give it gas with the right pedal."

I press down with my right foot and start easing out the clutch pedal—slow and steady. Or so I think. The bus lurches forward like a startled bull; its engine sputters, then goes silent. Shit, I killed Daisy.

"Smooth," Carter says.

"Shut up," I snap. I'm in no mood for his shit. My palms are slick, my heart pounding. "I've got this."

I push in the clutch and crank the ignition; the engine rumbles back to life. "Crutch, where's that video? Show it to me from the beginning."

Crutch rewinds the video and shows the startup sequence to me again. I nod. "Okay, I think I get it. Let's try this again."

This time, I ease the clutch out more slowly while pressing gently on the gas. The gear catches. The bus trembles and inches forward.

"Hell yeah," I mutter, releasing the clutch completely and increasing the gas. The bus gains speed. "Holy shit—I'm driving Miss Daisy!"

"Don't celebrate yet," Crutch says, his eyes flicking between the video and the dash, then he points at a dial. "Watch that dial, it's the tachometer. If hits the red, you've gotta shift to a higher gear."

"How do you do that?"

"Floor the clutch, then ease off the gas, then shift to second. Got it?"

"Yep," I reply, focusing on the gauges. The tachometer creeps toward the red, and the engine starts to scream. "Now!" Crutch exclaims.

I stamp the clutch, let up on the gas, and shove the gear shifter into second.

"Let the clutch out slow and give her some gas!" Crutch says.

The bus surges forward, the engine calming as we gain speed. Twenty-six. Twenty-eight. Thirty-four miles per hour.

"Woohoo! You've definitely got this, Max!" Sunshine cheers from the aisle.

"Keep going straight for now," Crutch says, bringing up the map on his screen. "You've got a turn coming up. I'll tell you when."

The tachometer needle climbs, flirting with the red zone. "Max! Shift again!" Crutch cries.

I shift smoothly into third. The engine hums in satisfaction as we cruise faster. Forty-four and climbing.

"Left at that bend coming up," Crutch says,

pointing out the windshield. "Then merge onto 376 south."

"You're clear on your right," Carter tells me.

I steer the bus into the turn, only to immediately realize that I'm going too fast. The bus flexes hard, groaning as it leans into the curve. I tighten my grip around the wheel, knuckles white as I fight to keep control of Daisy's vibrating shell. Tires screech, but I miraculously maintain control.

"Take it easy, Max!" Carter yells.

"Sorry! I'll get the hang of it."

Crutch tells me, "In two hundred miles, you'll hit a crossroad. Until then, keep straight."

Moonlight illuminates the empty, endless highway stretching out ahead of us. Daisy's engine growls steadily now, no longer sputtering or screaming. If I can keep this up, we might reach Snake Bend before the next sunset.

26. Walk Among Us

"Junior's already with them, Jim," Doc tells me as we trot toward the west wing. "He paged us. Didn't you hear him?"

"I was busy," I reply. "The seventy-seven are handled. You're welcome."

We round a corner and enter the west wing suite. Past the sitting room, Junior stands beside the master bedroom's entrance, his hulking body filling the doorframe. He raps loudly against the solid oak door with his knuckles as we approach.

"Come in!" Holtz's voice booms from the other side. Doc and I enter; Junior trails us in, closing the door behind us.

Inside, Louise Holtz perches at the foot of an enormous brass-frame bed. At its head, her husband reclines with a pillow propped behind his salt-and-pepper crew cut. Their twin boys are nestled beside him, while their youngest, Beth, is busy scrawling all over the cream-colored walls with crayons.

"You've been a busy boy, Jimbo," Holtz drawls. His voice is calm, almost amused. "And I'm grateful for everything you've done for my family."

"Thank you, sir," I say, bowing my head. "The honor is all mine. To serve you has filled me with humble joy and—"

Louise interrupts with a sharp laugh. "Ha! Humble joy? That's rich."

"M-ma'am?" I stammer, glancing nervously at Doc, who's fiddling with the collar of his lab coat. Junior grunts, offering no help.

Holtz fills the silence. "What my wife is trying to say, Jim, is that you sure know how to move a crowd."

"Thank you," I say, straightening up slightly.

"Great work with the seventy-seven who entered my house uninvited. Clean job, little mess. A job well done."

"Come again, sir?" I reply.

"You know what I mean. The seventy-seven."

"Of course, sir. It's the least I can do for all you've done for me." Did that weasel-fuck Doc Howson snitch? I told him to keep them on ice! I start to feel hot under my collar.

Louise snorts. "After all you've done for us,"

she mutters mockingly as she picks up a remote control. She clicks a button and a giant flat-screen on the wall opposite the bed flickers to life. The display splits into numerous digital squares, showing live feeds from what seem to be cameras scattered throughout the church. What the fuck? No one told about this.

One feed shows the operating room downstairs, another, the packed parking lot, and another, the baptismal chamber I just left. I spot one square that shows Samantha on the auditorium stage. Every goddamn corner of the church is under surveillance!

Holtz says mildly, "And now it all makes sense. You've been busy imprinting our new friends so that they respond to you and Samantha alone. Is that fair to say, Jim?"

My stomach flips. "Sir, I can explain. They need clear leadership to prevent chip malfunctions, and since you're focused on recovery, I thought—"

"Shut up, Jim. I'm tired of listening to your fucking nonsense!" Holtz waves his hand dismissively, then continues. "Now, since we're in a house of God, let's talk biblically, shall we? You're like Moses in this project I've named Exodus, while my family and I are God, Jesus, and the Holy Spirit, get me? This is our kingdom, Jim. We allow you to walk among us, eat our food, and breathe our air. But let's be clear—those are *my* essentials out there, and you serve *me*."

The twins taunt in unison, "You're just the help, Jim!"

Holtz continues. "We believe you've lost your way, Jim. Once again, your ego's gotten the best of you."

"Sir, how can I be lost when I follow you? I swear—"

"Jim!" Louise snaps. "Forget that. Tell me, where is your little sewer rat? I don't know whether to scold him or to congratulate him."

"Ma'am? I don't know. What do you—"

Their daughter Beth flings a crayon at me. I flinch; it bounces off my cheek. Little brat. She's a miniature version of Louise—same dark curls, same fiery eyes. "Mommy, he looks funny when he's nervous!" she exclaims. She sticks her tongue out at me.

"Jim!" Holtz barks, snapping my attention back to him. "Your sewer rat's disinformation campaign was too good—so good that Russia thought it was real! The kid even hacked into their top-level military networks. I tried to warn General Popov that it was all just my diversion tactic, but my call was too late. Russian military took out major USSF satellites in retaliation, and now we're in the beginning stages of a real goddamn war!"

"A real war, sir?" I whisper, stunned.

"Yes, goddamn it! Isn't it great?" Holtz says. He turns to one of the twins—I'm not sure which, I've never been able to tell them apart. "Coffee, son."

The boy scrambles off the bed, fills a mug from a carafe on a nightstand, and brings it to his father. Holtz sips deeply, then says, "I'm not worried about a war. Why, I have a small army, don't I? I own a fertile slice of paradise far away from the impending doom, and my army's going to protect it for me and my family. Even for you, Jimbo. That is, if you finish what you signed up for."

Holtz points toward the security camera feed of Samantha onstage. "And now, as an added bonus, I have *her*." He swings his pointer finger over and aims it at Doc. "And from what I understand, there's no telling how strong she'll become. Isn't that right, Howson?"

"Umm, yes. That's correct, sir," Doc says.

"Here's the deal, my boys," Holtz says. "Project Exodus must accelerate. We can't wait until tonight—we're leaving now."

"Now?" Doc blurts, growing red in the face. "The essentials aren't ready to travel! Their neural tissues are still too fragile. We need more time!"

"Enough!" Holtz roars. "I will not tolerate such pessimistic thinking, Howson!" He takes a deep breath and lowers his voice to continue. "We've been working together for a long time, you and I. Frankly, I've grown sick of hearing your voice. You whine too much. Why, where's your sense of adventure, man? Your ambition?"

Voice trembling, Doc says, "Sir, I'm just being realis—"

Holtz snaps his fingers, and Junior's gorilla-like hands shoot out, gripping the doctor by the throat. The veins in Doc's neck bulge as Junior squeezes tighter, and the old man wheezes pathetically for breath.

"Realistic, huh?" Holtz growls. "Let *me* be realistic, Doc—I'm having a hard time imagining living in paradise with you!"

Doc's face turns bright purple, and his eyes bulge out of their sockets.

"Sir!" My voice cracks over Doc's grunts. "We need him!"

"What the hell do I need him for?" Holtz snaps.

"He's the best surgeon we've got! Think of your family!" I don't mention it, but I need his help with bringing Samantha to her full potential, too.

Holtz sighs and nods to Junior, who lets go of Doc. The old guy drops to the floor. "Not another complaint out of you, Howson," Holtz warns. "If I ask you to jump, you ask me how high!"

"Yes ... sir," Doc manages to say between gasps.

"Fan-fuckin'-tastic," Holtz says, rubbing his hands together as if he's trying to start a fire. "I'm thrilled that we're all on the same page. Now, it's time for the final phase of Project Exodus to commence! .... God, I've been dying to say that all day. Son, coffee!"

27. No time to stop

I've had the speedometer pinned at seventy-three miles per hour for the last ten-plus hours. The fuel gauge is on its last tick, and the desert outside is a blur of beige. My vision has tunneled, narrowed to the endless stretch of road before us, and I feel fucking great. I'm *in the zone*.

We've kept off the major freeways for as long as we could, avoiding Las Vegas and taking a route through eastern California. It's mid-afternoon, and the sky is the clearest blue I've ever seen on an early spring day. We're getting close to the outskirts of Phoenix, and we'll swing south of it to reach Snake Bend.

We're getting close, but I can't ease up. Not yet, because Jim has my mother. *Why?* What does he want with her? Jim, what the hell are you up to?

Words that don't belong together swirl inside my head: *mother, Jim, Snake Bend.* Don't over-think it, Max. Focus on the road ahead!

We're cruising southeast on Salome Road, which crosses over the I-10 Eastbound from Los Angeles to Phoenix. From the overpass, I look down at a nightmare below us—bumper to bumper, cars jammed together tight, people leaning out of their windows screaming at each other, fists flying, guns flashing in the chaos.

I'm hit by a flashback of the morning Phase Zero began in Bellingham. Thank fucking good-ness our road is free of mayhem. We cross with ease and continue southeast.

"This will get us to the 85, then the 85 South should take us all the way to Snake Bend," Crutch says from the bench seat behind me, where he's been camped out on his laptop.

Salome Road guides us far from the ruckus and into the heart of agricultural land. Flat green fields emerge to either side, their vivid color a star-tling contrast to the khaki-toned landscape around them.

To my right, Carter's standing in the shallow stairwell, one hand holding onto a railing and the other holding his binoculars to his eyes. He got his neck on a swivel, scanning the terrain ahead. "Hey, that must be Phoenix," he says. "I see a shit-load of tall buildings way over there."

I glance over at him; he's got his binoculars pointed past me, toward the eastern horizon. "That means we're close to Snake Bend, less than an hour away. Crutch, when's my next turn?"

"It's coming up in—"

The sky flashes so bright, it's like the sun just burst open. I wrap an arm across my face and slam the brakes blind. Daisy screeches to a stop, and I hear bodies tumble across the floor behind me.

Carter yells, "What the fuck! I can't see!"

I cautiously raise my eyes from my elbow. Whatever that light was, it's gone. Carter's still in the stairwell, but he's dropped the binoculars and he's rubbing at his eyes frantically.

I swing my gaze to my left, and that's when I see it—a massive mushroom cloud is belching into the sky above Phoenix, its base glowing with red flames.

I rub my eyes to make sure I'm seeing things correctly. Fuck me, my eyes seem to be working just fine.

"I'm fucking blind! I can't see!" Carter keeps screaming.

"Hang on, I'm pulling over!" I tell him. I pull Miss Daisy over onto the dirt shoulder and kill the engine.

I hear footsteps from behind. "It's me, cuz," Sunshine says, hopping down into the stairwell. "Quit touching your eyes! Here, sit down on the stairs, let me have a look. Can you see anything at all?"

"I told you, I'm blind!"

"Any lights and shadows? Shapes?"

"Well ... yeah, I guess, but it's all super blurry."

"What's going on up there?" Chuck calls to us from the back, sounding groggy. He's sitting up, propped up on his elbows and peering toward us. I'm filled with relief—it's the first time he's been conscious since Sunshine knocked him out with that powder.

"There was a bright light," I tell him, "and now there's a mushroom cloud over Phoenix!"

"There's a what?" Chuck cries, sounding instantly more alert. "Everyone, duck and cover!"

"What do you—"

BAAAM!

An invisible wall of brute force slams me backward in my seat. I can't see a thing outside; dust has kicked up all around us. I drop to my stomach, flat on the floor, and wait there while winds howl and pelt the side of the bus with sand.

BOOOOOOM!

A monstrous roar rips through us. Daisy shivers violently as if she's having a seizure, her window glass rattling.

After a moment, the dust settles and the noises fade. I scramble to my feet. The sky is gray with ash, and the mushroom cloud has doubled in size. Fuck—it's true, we're under attack! Millions of people have just been vaporized! What other cities have been hit? Who the fuck did this?

Sunshine calls out, "Is everyone okay?" We all holler back that we're fine, except Carter, who shouts, "I'm fucking blind! Does that sound like I'm okay to you?!"

"Simmer down, cuz," Sunshine says. "Hey Crutch, do you have a flashlight? A headlamp, anything?"

"Here, catch!"

"Thanks, Crutch! Okay, Carter, hold still, let me check to see if your pupils dilate."

"That was a shockwave from a nuke, and pretty soon we're gonna see fallout," Chuck informs us. "Get this bus moving, get as far away from ground zero as you can!"

"Are you saying turn around?" I ask. Fuck! We were so goddamn close.

"Max, if we keep going straight, we'll hit the southbound route to Snake Bend in under a minute," Crutch says. "That will get us away from Phoenix."

I start up Daisy again and ease her back on the road. Chunks of fences and tree branches are scattered all over the pavement. I begin to maneuver the bus through the obstacles.

Sunshine announces, "There's no permanent

damage to Carter's eyes, from what I can tell. Can you see any better now, cuz?"

"A little."

"Good, just give it time. It might take a day or two."

We reach a T-junction. Crutch tells me, "Max, take the right." I blow past the stop sign and take the turn with confidence, fast and smooth.

Chuck yells, "Is Andretti driving up there? Holy mackerel!"

"It's me!" I tell him.

"Max? Since when do you know how to drive a stick?"

"It's been a long night, Chuck!"

We're southbound on the Old U.S. Highway 80. A sign announces an upcoming scenic view of the Snake River. Whatever, I don't give a shit. All I care about is getting to Snake Bend.

I will myself back into *the zone*. The world shrinks to a narrow tunnel ahead of me, and I focus on nothing but driving.

Driving ... I need ... to keep ... driving ...

Mother ... Jim ... Snake Bend ...

Behind me, I'm vaguely aware of my friends moving around, talking to each other, helping Chuck move up to a bench, but I concentrate on the road ahead.

Driving ... I need ... to keep ... driving ...

The sky above has darkened, and ash is falling all around us. I turn the windshield wipers on.

Mother ... Jim ... Snake Be—

At last, ahead I see a sign that reads: *Welcome to Snake Bend.* Tension ripples through my body as I slow the bus to twenty, rolling past sun-bleached manufactured homes and cars on cinderblocks. Snake Bend seems to be Arizona's version of Oak Falls. There's even a stray dog in the street—or is that a coyote?

I slow Daisy to a crawl. Her gas light's blinking, but there's no time to stop. There's no fill-up station in sight, anyway. "Where to now, Crutch?" I ask. "The video said they would be at some church, right?"

"Yeah, the Church of the Holy Desert," Crutch says. "I got it here on my map. Take this left, then go straight over the railroad tracks. Then the church should be up a few blocks on the right."

I take the left and see the railroad tracks up ahead. But wouldn't you know it, just before we reach them, lights flash from the crossing gate. A metal arm folds down, preventing our passage, and a high-pitched chime begins to ring out.

For a split second, I think about punching it, driving through the barrier—*Miss Daisy can take it*—but a more rational part of my brain convinces me that I might have run out of lives already. I bring the bus to a stop.

"There's a train coming!" I holler over the chime. "We have to wait. "

... and once the road is clear, then what? It hits me then that we don't have even an inkling of a plan. I've been so caught up driving in a trance, I've lost sight of the bigger picture. Jim, Mom, Snake Bend, sure, but what now?

Do I break down the church's front door using Miss Daisy like a battering ram? Or maybe we should find the local cops and tell them there's been a kidnapping, or ... I don't know, but I suppose we can figure out the details while we wait for the train to pass. That's enough time, right?

I turn around. The whole gang is camped out on the bench seats behind me, even Chuck. "Hey guys, now that we're here, what's next? What's our game plan?"

"The plan is to rescue your mom!" Sunshine replies.

"Okay, but how?" I ask.

"Well, I for one vote for covert ops," Chuck says. "I say we check out the church and stake it out until we know what's going on. Then we make our move."

Crutch says, "I can scout it out. Send me in."

"I can't let you do that alone," I protest.

A train whistle shrieks in the near distance. I turn back around to an unexpected sight. Across the tracks and up the block, a horde of people are marching toward us. They're packed together, clotting the entire street from sidewalk to sidewalk. Is this a protest, or a parade, or what?

And ... that's ... interesting. Leading the pack is a black, beat-to-hell SUV missing its front bumper, and it looks a hell of a lot like my Beast.

28. At My Pleasure

Five thousand and seven essentials await my command inside the auditorium, and I'm at a loss for words. I've lost my edge; the meeting's thrown me for a loop. They're not mine—they're his, hers, the Holtz family's! Ten thousand dilated eyeballs watch my every move as the essentials wait for me to speak. They're primed, and like a loaded gun, each of them is cocked and ready to fire on a single command. But I can't fucking pull the trigger.

Samantha says, touching my jacket sleeve, "Our children are ready for you."

Our children. She's right. No matter what Holtz says, these essentials are our children and ours alone.

"I love you, Samantha," I tell her.

"I love you too."

Get it together, Jim. Don't screw this up now. I bring the PA mic close to my lips and begin. "My essentials, the time has come for our exodus to paradise! Stand and come to me!"

"Yes, Father!"

They stand and march down the aisles without making as much as a peep. Silent killers they shall be. Obedient workers. My disciplined children, my army of essentials. They're all fucking mine! Mi—

The house of God begins to shake. The overhead lights swing wildly as if they might tear free from the rafters at any second.

"Earthquake!" I shout. "Follow me on the double!"

The essentials rush toward the stage. I grab my earpiece and yell, "Junior, Doc! Does anybody copy?"

Nothing but raspy static fills my ears, and I hurl the useless earpiece to the floor. "Samantha, grab some essentials to help you carry out all the medical equipment. Then find the Holtzes, find Junior and that goddamn Doc, and meet me in the parking lot!"

"Certainly, Jim," Samantha says. Before I can blink, she's gone, off to fulfill my wishes like a genie from a bottle.

The shaking stops as suddenly as it started. I look around; although a few essentials have stumbled to the floor, I don't see any major damage. I raise my hands above my head and yell, "All together now, single file! Follow me, my children!"

I lead them out the building through the emergency exit backstage. Outside, the sky glows blood-red. On the northeastern horizon, Phoenix—or what used to be Phoenix—is nothing but a towering mushroom cloud. We've been hit! Holy hell, the Russians aren't messing around! Looks like I'm the least of the FBI's worries now.

"Fall in!" I tell my essentials, and they huddle close together in the church parking lot. "Twenty lines deep!" I command, and they begin to form twenty even lines. As more and more essentials pour from the building, the lines grow until each stretches to the fence at the far end of the lot.

"Jim, what the fuck!"

I turn and see Samantha, Doc, the Holtz family, and Junior exiting the church.

Holtz continues, "Do you not see what's going on out here? Look at the sky, you fucking numbnut! Quit standing up with your thumb up your ass and get my essentials moving!"

"You useless idiot! They should be halfway to the loading zone by now!" Louise yells.

I keep my cool, exhaling through my nose, and on the inhale, I flash the Holtzes a smirk before giving the command: "Samantha, escort the Holtzes safely to my meat wagon, dear."

"Absolutely, Jim," Samantha says. Before they can react, she brusquely grabs the couple by their wrists and begins hauling them toward the Suburban.

"Let go of me, you bitch!" Louise screams. "Jim, she's hurting me!"

"Please, ma'am, just follow Samantha to our secure vehicle," I say sweetly. "We must lead the essentials to the loading zone. Isn't that what you want?"

Louise continues to swear at Samantha as she drags them away, the children trailing behind them.

"I'll see you soon," I say to the Holtzes, waving at them like I give a shit. "You too, Doc," I say. "Get in the ass end of the wagon."

Doc scurries after Samantha. Their feet leave smudges on the thin layer of ash covering the ground.

I turn to Junior, who's standing there like a fucking lump on a log. "You too, no-neck. I'll be right behind you."

He stares at me, blank-faced.

"You got a fucking problem, Junior?"

"No problem, Jim," Junior says.

"It's boss, remember?"

Junior grunts, "Sure, boss," and walks away.

Fuck him too. If Holtz has Junior's mind twisted on the facts, then I guess it's going to be me and my family against them—against the world!

I stop for a moment to admire the mushroom cloud on the horizon. It's doubled since I first stepped outside, and while some might tremble in terror, I revel in its glorious strength. Like it, I will unleash my power at my pleasure—when the time is right, I'll strike. I'll make them understand just how strong I am!

"My children!" I yell at the top of my lungs. "Follow me and stay in formation! March together as one!"

"Yes, Father!" they respond in unison.

I lead them through the parking lot to the meat wagon and slide behind the wheel. Samantha awaits me in the front passenger seat, while everyone else is crammed together in the back.

Immediately, Holtz barks, "Father, huh, Jim? I thought we talked about that?"

"I can't change their programming now, sir. It is what it is."

"We'll see about that," Holtz sneers. "Just drive us the hell out of here!"

"Yes, sir. I'm at your command," I tell him.

Chooo! Choooooooo!

A train howls outside. "Sounds like our ride is right on time," I say.

"Of course it is, Jim!" Holtz snaps. "I set up

the damn thing! Don't you forget who's really running the show around here."

"I won't forget, sir," I say. "Wouldn't forget for a second who's in charge." I tap my meat wagon's accelerator, and we ease away from the Church of the Holy Desert and on to the next destination.

Onward and upward! My heart flutters as we exit the parking lot and onto the street. I'm going to miss this church, but soon, I'll possess a new kingdom many times as grand, many times as fit for a God! Soon, I will reign in paradise with my queen!

29. The Cheapest Crowns

Is that my old whip? I can't say for sure— it's hard to tell from this distance, especially without a side view.

I can't make out the faces in the front seat either. I squint as the SUV rolls toward us at a crawl, followed by a mob of people. I yell, "Carter, you still got those binoculars?"

"I dropped them up there, after I got blinded!" Carter says.

I look down, and luckily they've rolled to the base of the captain's chair. I snatch them up and peer through the eyepieces.

Sunshine walks up to the front and gasps. "What are all those people doing in the middle of the street? ... Are those medical beds they're carrying?"

"What people?" Carter asks. "Goddamnit,

everything is still blurry! Max, somebody, talk to me! Are we under attack or what?"

I ignore them for the moment and scan with the binoculars until I've locked onto the windshield of the Suburban. And there! Behind the steering wheel, I see him—Jim! Jim with that awful shit-eating grin, and at his side ... it's her! That's my mother!

Then, the SUV slows before the train tracks and turns onto a side road, revealing the stamp alongside her body that reads: MEAT WAGON #4.

"JIM! You mother-snatching Beast-stealing fuckface, Jim! I'm coming for you!" I scream. I throw the binoculars aside and jam the shifter into gear. Guess we're going to break through the safety bar after all.

And just as I'm about to slam the accelerator to the floor, a whistle blows and a freight train's locomotive hurtles by. It's followed by graffiti-covered boxcars, one after another, and through the cracks between each car, I catch snapshots of the back of my Beast as it drives away, parallel with the tracks. The marchers follow it down the road.

"Goddamnit!" I bellow. "FUCK! FUCK!" I stand and begin to pace up and down the aisle. I'm so pissed, I can't think straight. Seeing Jim for that micro-second has got me all hot and bothered.

And thanks to this train, he's getting away with my mother! "One stupid minute too slow, and now they're gone!" I moan.

Sunshine reaches out and grabs my elbow as I storm past her for the third time. "Hey! Are you sure, Max?" she asks. "One hundred percent sure that was Jim? Was your mom with him?"

"Yes, I'm sure!" I snap, trembling. "That was him, *and* my mom, *and* my Beast! Look at me! My nerves are fired up! I'm about to explode!"

"Max, buddy," Chuck says. "Take it easy, kid. You'll be no good on the fighting field if your nerves are all out of whack."

I take a deep breath. "You're right, Chuck," I say. "Sorry, Sunshine, I shouldn't have snapped at you like that. And yes, I'm positive. I saw what I saw."

Chuck looks straight at me, then tilts his head toward the captain's chair. "Max, you've got us this far, and now you're going to get us across the finish line. We'll get your mother back! That's a promise."

"Thanks, Chuck," I tell him. I take a few more deep breaths, trying to calm my pounding heart. As I do, a sudden gratitude overwhelms me. They're being so patient with me, and they've all stood by me this entire journey. None of them had to come all this way with me for my mother.

"Thanks to all of you, Carter, Sunshine, Crutch—thank you, I mean it."

Crutch nods at me and smiles.

"Don't mention it," Sunshine responds. "And don't worry, Max. When the tracks are clear, gun it and we'll catch up."

Carter says. "Just wait until my vision comes back! I'm going to destroy that fucktard Jim for messing with my brother!"

I climb back into the captain's chair. The train begins to slow, its brakes squeaking. The time between passing boxcars becomes longer and longer, letting us see more and more of the horde and my Beast as they move farther and farther away.

The final train car passes us, and a moment later, the safety arm bar retracts. I fire up old Daisy's engine and cry out, "Hold on!" We lunge forward for a split second before the RPM needle drops to zero. I stomp on the gas, but there's no power, and Daisy coasts over the tracks on the fumes of her final gasp.

"Whoa, did the engine give out?" Carter asks.

The fuel gauge needle is well below its last tick. "Nope. We're out of gas," I reply as I guide Daisy onto the side road, where her momentum runs out.

"So what now? Do we hoof it?" Sunshine asks.

"Gang, we have activity up ahead," Chuck says.

The Beast and its parade of followers must be a mile down the road. From here, the people are the size of ants, and my Beast seems no larger than a Micro Machine.

"The train stopped," Sunshine says.

"Yes, and look at that," Chuck says. "They're climbing aboard, whoever they are."

I bring the binoculars to my eyes once more. He's right; his eyes must be as sharp as an eagle's. Thousands of people are filing into the train, and doing so with startling efficiency. Within moments, most of them have distributed themselves among the boxcars. A group of them surround the Beast, like ants swarming a cookie to collectively move an object a thousand times their weight.

"What do you see, Max?" Sunshine asks.

"Um, those people just picked up my Beast and put it on a flatcar," I say. "And like Chuck said, they're all boarding the train. But I don't see Jim or my mom anywhere. They're not in the Beast; maybe they've already boarded."

Who the hell are all these strange people, and where is Jim hiding my mother? A sickening thought hits me like a lightning bolt. Are all these people *chipped*? Like all those horrible deputies in the Oak Falls High auditorium? Like what Jim did to Sunshine, controlling her as he wished? Fuck, did he chip my mother?

"Come on, what are we waiting for?" Carter cries. "We've got a train to catch!" He springs up, takes one step, and trips, falling to his knees.

"Are you okay?" Sunshine says, helping her cousin to his feet.

"Yeah, I'll be fine. Just tell me which way I should run."

Chuck says, "Son, you ain't running anywhere."

"What? I'm going, I just need a hand is all, and—"

"Not today," Chuck cuts him off. "Max, this old dog and his blind son are gonna stay right here."

"No way, Pops! I came all this way, I'm not—"

"Stop that nonsense, Carter," Sunshine says. "Look, your Pops is in no shape to be running after a train car. He's still recovering, and he needs you to stay here and take care of him, okay?"

"That's right," Chuck says. "I need you, son. Max and the rest need to catch up with that train and jump on before it takes off. I know I can't do it, and a man's gotta know his limits in life, get me?"

Carter slumps. "Brother, I'm sorry," he mumbles to me. "My Pops needs me."

"It's okay," I tell him. "But listen, guys. All

those people getting into the train? What if they're chipped, and under Jim's control?"

Crutch pushes off his bench and runs to the back. "I'll be right back!" he calls out.

"I'm with you," Sunshine tells me. "I don't care what we're up against. We're getting your mom back." She turns to Carter and hands him her phone. "Here, cuz, take this."

"I thought you weren't getting any signal," Carter says.

"Crutch fixed it up earlier," Sunshine explains. "He synced it up with Max's somehow. Right, Crutch?"

"Yeah, got 'em geosynchronized," Crutch says. "I've got Max's right here. We can use them to keep in touch."

I take a deep breath. "I don't know how we're going to pull this off without you two, but I guess we're going to have to. Goodbye, Jacksons!"

"Put it here, partner," Chuck says, sticking his hand at me for a shake.

I knock his hand aside, lean in, and hug the big guy instead. His mighty arms wrap around my shoulders.

"Take care of my niece, will ya?"

"Sure thing," I tell him.

"I love you, Uncle Chuck," Sunshine says, "Max, we gotta leave now if we're gonna make that train!"

The train whistle blows twice, and the box cars' wheels begin to roll.

Crutch dashes past us, backpack over his shoulders. He pauses at the door to yell, "Hurry up! That train is leaving!" Then he's out the bus and sprinting toward the train.

"This is not goodbye, Max," Carter says. "No way. We'll see you again."

I tell him, "We will, brother." He pushes his fist out for a bump, and we tap knuckles. Then Sunshine and I are out the door, hauling ass after Crutch down the middle of the train tracks.

Crutch is the first to reach the slow-moving train, and he hops aboard a small platform jutting from the final boxcar. Sunshine is next, and Crutch reaches out and helps pull her up.

I stumble; the railroad ties are uneven, with loose gravel between them. The train is picking up speed, and I'm running out of it!

"Come on, Max!" Sunshine cries out. "Take my hand!" She leans far out, one hand holding onto the railing surrounding the platform and the other outstretched toward me. "Jump, Max!" she hollers.

The train whistles as it gains more speed. It's now or never. I take one, two, three more strides and leap into the air, reaching for Sunshine's hand. "Gotcha!" she says, yanking me into her with one big heave-ho. We tumble onto the plat-form, safe and sound.

"Nice job, you two," Crutch says, taking a seat on the metal floor beside us as we catch our breath.

Behind us, the mushroom cloud still hovers menacingly on the horizon, but our distance from it is growing. It frames the sight of Chuck and Carter leaning out of Miss Daisy's door, waving. I wave back, then the train rounds a bend, and they're gone from view. A bleak part of my mind wonders if I'll ever see them again.

I stand and assess our situation. There's just enough room on this platform for all three of us, and if it weren't for the railing I'm gripping, I'd be freaking out. I've never hitched a ride on a train before; how fast do these things go? Is this platform the best place to be when it's moving at full speed?

I carefully turn around. There's a metal ladder welded to the back of the boxcar that leads up to the roof, and next to it is a small door. "We should try to get inside," I say, giving the door handle a tug. "Fuck, it's locked."

Sunshine stands and tries the handle as well, twisting and tugging it, but it doesn't budge.

"I'll see if there's another way in," Crutch says. Before we can respond, he's already up the ladder and on top of the boxcar, then out of sight.

The train lets out another screech, and we speed up to what feels like forty—maybe fifty—miles per hour. The ground below blurs.

"Guys!" Crutch yells. "There's a hatch!"

Sunshine hollers back, "Can you open it?"

A moment passes with no reply. Just as I'm about to yell out his name, Crutch's ginger head pokes over the edge. He turns around and climbs back down to the platform.

"Did you get it open?" I ask him.

"Yeah," he says, rubbing sweat off his forehead with the back of his hand.

"Great, so can we fit through it? Let's get inside. I, for one, don't enjoy this dinky platform. It feels like it's gonna fall off any second!"

"There's no room for us, Max. It's packed like a tin of sardines. And even if there were, I still wouldn't go in there."

"What are you saying, Crutch?"

"They're chipped. Everyone inside is chipped."

"Are you sure?"

"I saw the backs of their necks with my own eyes, Max."

"Jesus, there must be thousands of them on this train," Sunshine mutters.

How the fuck did Jim gather *thousands* of them?

"Maybe we could make this work *for* us,"

Crutch says. "Check this out." From his backpack, he pulls out the yellow clamshell lockbox from his trailer. He pops it open and pulls out a silver box the size of a deck of cards.

"What is that?" Sunshine asks. "Some kind of remote?"

"Kind of," he replies. He extends its collapsed antenna. On the face of the device is a monochromatic screen with a bunch of buttons below it. I know what this is. I've seen it before. Hell, I've used it before!

"It's the transmitter from Oak Falls High," I say. "Isn't it?"

Crutch nods, grinning widely. "Want me to check if it still works? I haven't had a chance to try it, but it's fully charged."

"Yeah!"

Crutch powers it on, points it toward the door, and presses a button. We wait, but it's quiet inside the boxcar.

"I don't get it," Sunshine says. "What's supposed to happen?"

"They should be ripping each other's heads off, tearing each other from limb to limb!" Crutch replies.

"Try it again," I tell Crutch. "Are you sure you're pushing the right button?"

"I'm sure. I know how this thing works. I need to run some diagnostics. Here, Max, hang onto it for a second." He hands me the transmitter and begins to dig within his backpack.

Sitting cross-legged on the platform, Crutch lifts his laptop from his bag and settles it on his lap. "Let me see that again, Max," he says. I hand him the transmitter; he connects it to his laptop with a cable and begins to type away at a gazillion words per minute.

"Let us know if you need anything, Crutch," Sunshine says.

The kid mumbles, "Okay," his eyes glued to the screen.

Sunshine and I sit with our backs against the boxcar. The train traces a curve to the southeast, through an endless lonely desert dotted with thorny bushes and otherworldly cacti. To one side, way out in the distance, are jagged, rock-capped mountain tops. To the other, the sun is setting, streaking golden rays against the sands.

The quiet landscape repeats itself over and over—more cacti, another dry mountain. The train is picking up speed, and I let out a big breath stemmed from the frustration and total utter fucking confusion from the past days.

Sunshine must have heard me; she sets her hand on my knee. "It will be okay," she says. "We'll get her back."

I nod and thank her. She closes her eyes and I

continue to stare out into the bleak, dry surroundings.

After what feels like an hour, Crutch is still hammering away on his keyboard while Sunshine is dead to the world, sprawled out like roadkill beside me. For the first time since we ditched Snake Bend, there's a flicker of life beyond the dirt and emptiness. To my right, the faint outlines of towns claw up from the horizon.

Then, the billboards start popping up. Big, faded ones, their Spanish slogans peeling under years of sun and wind. Tequila. Restaurants. Dentists promising the cheapest crowns this side of the border. Far off, a semi-truck lumbers along a dusty highway.

We pass a Mexican flag—bright and defiant—flapping from the side of a squat brick building. And just like that, it hits me like a sucker punch to the gut.

Holy shit, we're in Mexico.

"¡Viva la México!" I say.

"What, Max?" Sunshine says, stretching her arms and legs like a barn cat soaking up the midday sun. "Mexico?" She sits up and rubs the sleep out of her eyes.

"Yeah, we must have crossed the border, look!"

I point at yet another building with a green, white, and red flag as we hurtle past it.

"You weren't kidding. Viva la México, Max."

We need to use whatever remaining time we have left to cook up a solid game plan. We have to be sneaky. Covert ops, like Chuck said. We can't get caught ... but all those chipped people following Jim ... how the fuck did he do it?—wait!

"Hey, listen up, I have an idea," I tell them. "Whenever this train stops, I'm assuming that the cargo will unload. There's thousands of them, right? So let's blend in, pretend we're one of them, and go wherever they go. We'll stay in the middle of the horde so we don't get made, try to figure out where Jim's keeping my mom, and when the timing is perfect, we'll get—"

ROOOOOOOOAAAAAAARRRRRRRR!

A huge, low-flying plane passes right over us. Damn, that thing was close.

"Use the essentials as cover. Copy that," Crutch says, still typing away.

"Essentials?" Sunshine asks.

"Yeah, that's what Jim called them," Crutch replies, looking up at us. "Something about their organs and blood being essential."

Sunshine shudders, then says, "Max, do you think Jim chipped your mom? That must be it, right? Why else would she stay with him?"

"I think you're right," I tell her. "We'll know once we can get close to her. If she is, we'll get that chip out of her."

I peer around the side of the platform, toward the front of the train. Way ahead, there's a sign; I have to squint my eyes to see it. I read out loud, "Bienvenido al Aeropuerto Internacional."

"Welcome to the International Airport," Sunshine translates. We look at each other, lost for words. Our eyelids flutter as if this new information has fried our brains.

"Airport?" Crutch says.

Sure enough, the train tracks lead straight into an airport. Ahead of us, I see several grounded planes—they look like military cargo planes, with camouflage paint jobs.

The train whistle shrieks, and after a few minutes, the train cars rattle to a stop near the tarmac. I lean out over the platform's railing and scan for the flatcar holding my Beast, but I don't see it anywhere.

Just as I stretch my neck out further for a better look-see, all the boxcars' loading doors open in unison. Essentials begin pouring from the boxcars and onto the cracked pavement. They move efficiently, keeping close together like one massive organism.

My neck retracts back like a frightened turtle's. "Are you two ready?" I ask. "It's time to go." My heart's thudding hard against my ribs.

"Just a second, Max," Crutch says, his fingers flying frantically over his keyboard.

Sunshine joins me at the railing. "There's so many of them ... wait!" she cries. "Is that your Beast, way over there?"

She's right. I spot my baby in the distance, heading straight toward us and the growing swarm of essentials on the tarmac. "Get down," I tell her.

"Follow me!" Jim's voice cries out, amplified. "Follow me, my essentials!"

Crouching down, I peer past the essentials and see Jim hanging out the Beast's driver's side window, screaming through a bullhorn. And sitting next to that fucker again is my mother.

"Follow me to paradise!" Jim yells. He points at a ginormous plane parked behind him, its cargo bay open like a yawning mouth.

"Let's go," Crutch says, tightening his JanSport's straps around his shoulders.

"Did you get the transmitter working?" I ask.

"There's only one way to find out."

"Not now, Crutch," I say. "First, we need to blend with the essentials and try to get closer to my mom. Follow my lead."

I make my move first, climbing down from the train platform and tiptoeing to the edge of the horde. I hear footsteps behind me as Sunshine and Crutch follow. We elbow ourselves into the mix. I'm nervous at first, but relax as I realize that none of these chipped people seem to notice or care about our presence.

"Attention!" Jim yells. "Form lines!"

Like in a well-rehearsed dance, the essentials swiftly organize themselves into many columns of neat, single-file lines. I manage to snag a spot in one of them, and Sunshine and Crutch slip into lines on either side of me.

"Forward, march!" Jim yells.

We march forward with the essentials, keeping pace as they follow the Beast toward the huge plane. As we get closer to the aircraft, I see a wide loading ramp stretching down to the tarmac, looking like the tongue of a metal giant. The Beast disappears up the ramp and into the belly of the plane, then re-appears, now facing toward us.

The doors to the Beast swing open, and people spill out like a clown car—some I've only seen before on TV or social media. There's Louise Holtz, the ex-Governor of Washington, and her coffee-tycoon husband. The last time I saw them, they were on TV in orange jumpsuits. Their kids are with them, though I can't remember their names.

And then there's Dr. Howson, his white hair glowing under the lights. That quack colluded with the Holtzes in their Washington cover-up scandal. Fucking crazy old bastard! Next to him stands a refrigerator with arms and legs—Junior! The no-neck psycho who almost killed me!

Jim steps out from the driver's seat and waves

at his army of essentials. "Load up!" he yells, pointing into the cargo bay. "It's going to be a tight fit, but you'll manage! And when we land together in paradise, it will all have been fucking worth it!"

My mother climbs out from the passenger side and walks over to Jim. He wraps his stinkin' arm around her shoulder and plants a fat, juicy kiss on my mother's lips! What the fuck is going on around here?!

My fists ball up, and all I want to do is run up and tackle that sonofabitch, pound his face over and over again until his smirk is nothing but a bloody—

"Be cool, Max," Sunshine whispers to me. "We can't give our position away now."

The essentials continue marching toward the plane, forcing us along with them. I keep my eyes glued to my mother as she walks with Jim and the others down the ramp. They make their way toward the front of the plane, and I'm still too far back to do a damn thing about it. I watch as she disappears up a set of stairs into the plane's passenger cabin.

The wave of essentials carries us up the ramp. Once in the cargo bay, I break toward the parked Beast, signaling for Sunshine and Crutch to follow. I pop open her back doors, and we climb into the cool interior of my long-lost Suburban.

The last of the essentials cram into the bay.

They're packed so tight, I don't think I could open the Beast's doors if we needed to get out, and even if we could, where would we go?

The cargo hatch groans shut, echoing like a steel coffin sealing tight, and a harsh artificial light floods the cavernous bay. The jet engines scream to life with a ferocious roar, and the plane lurches down the airstrip, picking up tremendous speed. My body tenses as the the frame of the Beast trembles. The nose of the plane tilts up, and—we're airborne!

"Holy shit, guys," Crutch says, grinning. "We're flying! I've never flown before."

Me neither. I've never had the guts to board one of these death traps before. Now we're ripping through the sky, heading toward ... what did Jim say? Paradise?

30. Shook, Rattled, and Rolled

"Mommy, that one looks like a big ice cream cone!" Beth squeals with her face pressed against the plane window. "Look! Mommy, look at that one—it's huge!"

"Yes, dear, I see them," Louise says as she flips through the pages of a People magazine. "Why don't you take a seat and buckle up, okay?"

Beth lets out a sigh, then peels her face from the glass and shoves herself into her seat, where her short legs dangle above the floor. Her neck craned, she continues to stare out the window, rapt.

What has her so entranced is the moonlit horizon to the north, littered with nuclear mushroom clouds. Dozens of them, all in various sizes; some hang low, while others reach the outer limits of the biosphere. But all share the same general shape—from however many thousands of feet we're up at now, the mushroom clouds do resemble unholy ice cream cones, toxic treats not consumable by any living being!

"Mommy, where do ice cream clouds come from?" Beth asks.

Her mother folds her magazine in half and rests it against the thigh of her crossed leg. "Beth, honey, I'm not going to sugarcoat it for you. You're old enough to hear it, and I'd rather be the one to tell it to you, not some feeble-minded news reporter. You remember what Mommy and Daddy told you about reporters, right?"

"Yeah, I remember, Mommy!" Beth exclaims. "They're bad people and liars!"

"Yes, honey, they're liars. And liars get what they deserve! Beth dear, those aren't ice cream cones—they're billows of hot ash from bombs sent to punish the liars, liars like those bad reporters and the FBI men and that mean judge who locked Mommy and Daddy away. They're all dead because they hurt Mommy and Daddy!"

"Dead?" Beth asks. "Because they're bad people who hurt you?"

"Yes, sweetie. Those people down there were bad."

"But what about all those people on our plane, Mommy? Are they bad or good?" Beth asks, sounding troubled.

"Our essentials are good, honey. They believe in Mommy and Daddy."

"But they're weird," Beth says. "They don't look like they're happy."

"They might not show it, sweetie, but those people in our plane are very happy. They're happy because your Daddy and I, we're giving them a purpose and a beautiful paradise to live in. Beth, dear, we're saving those people, and when we get to our destination, you'll see. You'll understand why we worked so hard for all these years. Remember how Mommy worked hard to get our family into the Governor's Mansion?"

"Yeah, I do, the big white one! I miss it! I miss my room!" Beth cries.

"Me too, honey. But soon, we'll have a new house and it will be ten times larger and your room will be filled with all the toys you could ever want!"

"You mean it?" Beth asks.

"I do, darling," Louise says. She pats her daughter's head, caressing her curly hair. "When we land, we'll be treated like royalty, which makes you a princess. We're not far, so why don't you try to sleep like your brothers and Daddy?"

"Okay, Mommy, I'll try," Beth says, adjusting her seat to a reclining position.

"Good girl," Louise says. She unfolds her magazine and continues to flip through its pages.

I'm sitting across the aisle from Louise and Beth, with Holtz and the twins in front of them. In the window seat next to me, Samantha's been unresponsive for several hours, her eyes shut tight and her body rigid. This had me worried at first, and I asked Doc, "What's up with Samantha?"

The old man told me, "Her systems are undergoing optimization, Jim. She's stable. If you really need her, issue the wake command and she'll respond."

Doc and Junior are in the seats behind me, fast asleep. I've tried to catch a few winks of sleep, but I can't. I'm thrumming with anticipation about our arrival in paradise.

The plane shakes from what I hope is merely turbulence. The fasten-your-seat-belt signs light up, and Samantha's head smacks against my shoulder. Holtz and his boys wake and let out confused yelps. Beth screams, and Louise shushes her. And just as fast as the plane began to shake, it smooths out again.

Static crackles from the cabin speakers, then a man with a thick Russian accent announces, "Zis is captain speaking. Apologies for turbulence. Soon we reach destination."

The seat belt light shuts off, and I carefully reposition Samantha's head back to her headrest. Her eyes remain shut. I can't wait until we land this stupid thing.

I fucking hate planes. I've only flown once before—years ago, on a regional redeye from Bellingham to Spokane for a Gravediggers Expo. I had to be there lickety-split; I was a special guest, so there was no way around it. I loathed that buzzy little death trap. The squirmy fucker shook, rattled, and rolled over the Cascades, nearly giving me a panic attack.

This metal bird is many times the size of that fuckin' coffin with wings, but that doesn't change how much I despise being this high up. Even more so, I can't stand not being in control. Put me behind the wheel of whatever and I'm golden, but this? Moving at six-hundred-plus miles per hour at the mercy of two dipshit pilots I've never met—fuck off! Well, at least it won't last much longer.

My eyes wander around the cabin, and Louise catches my gaze from across the aisle. Her eyes narrow as we stare at each other for an awkward moment. God, I can't stand that woman. She's always had it in for me for some reason. She rolls her eyes and lets out a guff, then raises her shitty magazine as if I'm not worthy to look upon her face.

"Jim, get your ass over here!" Holtz hollers.

Fucking hell, what now? I unbuckle my belt, move up the aisle, and take the empty seat beside Holtz. I wait for him to speak first.

His twin sons are in the seats across the aisle.

One has his eyes closed; the other is drawing on a pad of paper with crayons. "Look," the kid says, holding up his drawing.

On the paper is a stick figure that I think is supposed to represent yours truly: dark hair, clean-shaven with a black suit. His eyes are bugged out of his head like Tex Avery's Wolfy cartoon, and the kid has scribbled yellow and red flames all around him. The little shit stares straight at me and says, "This is your fate."

Before I can reach over and snatch that piece of paper from him, crumple it up, and stuff it down his gullet, Holtz says, "Jim, I just wanted to say that you did a hell of a job with Project Exodus."

"Why, thank you, sir." I turn to him and beam, forgetting about the boy's stupid drawing.

Holtz continues, "We're getting close. After we land this baby, you're going to instruct my essentials to load up."

"Load up in what, sir?"

"There will be buses waiting for them. You'll see."

"And then what, sir?"

"My guys will escort us to paradise. Wait 'til you see my Humvee, what a ride! You and Samantha will come with us. Junior and Doc can bring up the rear in that beat-to-hell meat wagon of yours and make sure there are no stragglers."

"How long will it take to reach paradise from the airport?"

"Jesus fuckin' H. Christ on a cross, Jim. You ask more damn questions than my kids. If you must know, under an hour, okay? And since we're on the topic, let me break down how the rest of the day's gonna play out. When we get there, I need all my essentials gathered around—I've prepared a speech. And when I give the next orders, I need you to convey them verbatim to my new essentials. That's how it's gonna go until Doc fixes this verbal command horseshit. Got me, Jimbo?"

"I understand, sir. Except ... what are the next orders?"

Holtz ignores my question and leans back in his seat. "Jim, look out my window." I peer out past Holtz to a breathtaking view. A full moon illuminates ocean waves splashing against a rocky shore below. Further inland, rolling hills surround a sprawling city. Beyond the city lies a sparkling lake and an endless jungle cloaked with heavy fog.

The pilot's voice cuts in and says, "Zis is Captain. Please, prepare for landing." The plane begins a steep descent.

I start to pull back, but Holtz grabs my shoulder and stops me. "Before you go, Jim, I want you to see this," Holtz urges. "Take a good look, my boy—my empire is greater than you ever imagined."

Below, a massive, brightly lit billboard comes into view, towering above a hilltop overlooking the city. Plastered upon it is a giant photo of Holtz. He's depicted from the waist up, wearing army camouflage, with a fatherly smile upon his chiseled features and a steaming mug in his hand. Bold letters next to him proclaim: EL REY DEL CAFÉ.

"The King of Coffee," Holtz says proudly. "That's me—don't you fucking forget it. Welcome to Nicaragua, Jim. Go on and take your seat."

31. As you wish

In the back of the Beast, we count down in unison like it's New Year's Eve and the ball is about to drop—"Four, three, two, one!"

Crutch presses a button on the transmitter—click! The moment of truth—we wait for chaos to break loose outside the Beast, but nothing happens. The essentials just stand there pressed up against each other, eerily silent.

Crutch presses the button again. Still nothing.

"So they're supposed to be thrashing and bashing each other, right?" Sunshine asks.

"Yeah, they should be tearing into anything within reach," I reply, frustration creeping into my voice.

"Something's off," Crutch mutters. He runs a hand through his red hair, looking frazzled.

Here we are, packed inside a military cargo

plane and surrounded by thousands of chipped brains, soaring toward some so-called paradise. At some point, we're going to have to land. When we do, Jim and his goons will be there, and we're fucking unarmed and outnumbered a thousand to one. I rub my temples, feeling the weight of it all pressing down.

In a panic, I begin scouring the shelves in the Beast. They're chock-full of medical gear: wraps, tubes, gloves, cotton balls, IV bags, and blankets. Nothing that would help us against an army of essentials.

"The battery's full, the antenna's fine, and I soldered that broken wire," Crutch says, scrutinizing the transmitter. "The rest of the wiring looks good. The firmware is up and running. I guess I could run a few more diagnostics on the motherboard. Sunshine, can you toss me my backpack?"

Sunshine says, "Sure," and heaves the JanSport over to where Crutch is sitting. It lands on its side, spilling out a tangled web of cables, and something caught within the cables catches my eye.

"What's that?" I ask Crutch, pointing.

His eyes widen. "My Playstation controller. I didn't know that was in there. It's wireless!" He tugs it free from the cables and begins fiddling with it.

"Uh, guys?" Sunshine says. "Is this the best time to be playing games?"

"No games," Crutch replies. "I'm going to swap out the RF module from the transmitter and replace it with this controller's Bluetooth transceiver."

He connects the wireless controller to his laptop with a cable and begins to hammer on his keyboard. "Then I'll remap these inputs to real signals. If the transmitter used RF, we'll replace it with an NRF24L01 module. If it's infrared, we'll use an IR LED. If it's Wi-Fi, we'll send HTTP requests."

"Wait—Crutch, speak English," I say.

"I'll flip the PlayStation controller's signals into whatever the transmitter needs," Crutch explains. He unzips a side pocket on his backpack and pulls out a green object the size of a stick of gum. "And this little guy will help me do it."

"What is it?" Sunshine asks, squinting at it.

"A Raspberry Pi Zero, optimized for wireless."

"Sounds promising. How much time do you need?" I ask.

"Beats me. I've never done this before." Crutch hunches over the Playstation controller and starts taking it apart. Soon, he's lost in deep focus.

Sunshine and I exchange worried glances, and she scoots closer to me. "Okay, best-case scenario, let's say Crutch gets the transmitter to work," Sunshine says to me in a low voice. "The plane lands, Crutch presses the attack button, and the essentials start ripping each other to shreds. But I can't help thinking, what if they turn on us? Or on your mother?"

I've been trying to stay positive, but the thought has also crossed my mind. "You're right—we have no idea how these essentials will react," I tell her. "Sure, they'll create a distraction, but they could just as easily harm us. That's why we need to stay inside the Beast, where we'll be safe from the ruckus. I'll drive straight to my mother, grab her, and we'll get out of there."

Sunshine nods. "One problem, though," she says. "How are you driving without the car key?"

Out of instinct, I pat my jeans pockets, even though I know what I'll find: no key. However, my fingers brush against something else in the fifth pocket—Noah's gift. Great, like that's gonna start the Beast.

I move toward the front and peer through the perforated metal wall separating the cab from the rear. Well, what do you know? Lying on the driver's seat is the Beast's key. "Finally, some good lu—"

The plane tilts violently, the nose dropping fast. I tumble into Crutch. "Oh shit, we're crashing!" I yell.

My ears pop from the sudden pressure shift. My eyes squeeze shut—

THOOOMP!

The plane's tires slam into the ground and bounce erratically, then the whole thing shudders to a halt. I roll off Crutch, who doesn't even seem to notice that anything happened; he's busy dissecting the Playstation controller into pieces.

A deep metallic hiss fills the cargo space, and the hatch begins to lower. We've arrived.

Sunshine joins me, and we take in the view through the Beast's windshield. Outside, artificial lights illuminate a small landing strip with school buses parked alongside it. These buses look a hell of a lot like Miss Daisy, at least in shape and size. They're painted with wild colors and scenes, like the Virgin Mary praying next to a character from Dragon Ball Z.

One bus catches my eye. Splashed in bright red paint on its side are the words: PROPERTY OF HOLTZ COFFEE—EL REY DEL CAFÉ.

"The King of Coffee," Sunshine murmurs.

A military Humvee comes into view and stops at the bottom of the loading ramp. Jim shoves his head out the back passenger window, his greasy slicked-back hair shimmering under the runway lights. He shouts through a bullhorn, "Essentials! We have arrived! Now, exit the plane and load into the buses! Follow me to paradise!"

The essentials pour from the belly of the plane, down the ramp, and into the buses in neat, orderly rows. Within moments, the buses are packed to the gills, leaving the plane empty—except for us inside my Beast. The Humvee peels away, the buses following close behind, kicking up dust that blurs our view.

I turn toward Crutch; he's connecting his gadgets together with various cables and wires. "How's it coming? Need a hand?"

Crutch shakes his head.

"Max—incoming!" Sunshine hisses.

I pivot. At the bottom of the loading ramp, trouble approaches—Junior and Howson, striding straight for us.

"Get down," she whispers.

Sunshine and I hunker down on either side of Crutch. I grab a medical blanket from a shelf and drape it over us. The last thing I see before pulling it over our heads is Junior at the driver's door.

The Beast's front doors creak open, and her suspension drops from the added weight of new passengers from both sides. The doors shut with heavy thuds, sealing our fate—trapped in the Beast with couple of fucking psychopaths.

The Beast's engine fires up, and the sound of her V8 rumble brings me to tears. Oh, how I've missed her! She lurches down the ramp and onto the ground below.

The doctor's voice filters to us from the front. "Junior, now that we're alone, I have to tell you something. I don't think this old man can keep his charade up much longer."

"What are you talking about? We're here, Doc. We made it to paradise. So what's the problem?"

"Holtz wants me to override the essentials' voice control programming."

"Yeah, so? You told him you'll do it after we land."

"I realize that, but the thing is—there is no override option. I lied! And now he expects me to get it done as soon as possible!"

"Why can't it be done? We brought all that medical equipment from the church, right?"

"Yes, but it has nothing to do with equipment. It has to do with the fact that these new chips have fused themselves into the cellular structure of each essential! Samantha embedded nanotechnology into their design—the likes of which I've never seen! There's no way to override them or even to remove one without killing its host!"

"Goddamnit," Junior grumbles. "Why did you lie to Holtz in the first place?"

"I was stalling. I was trying to give myself more time."

"Well, you're still needed. Who else would replace his family's faulty livers?"

"I'm not the only surgeon in Nicaragua! I didn't get to my advanced age by ever making the mistake of thinking I'm irreplaceable."

"So, what are you going to do now?"

"I'll keep stalling him, and hopefully I can keep up the lie for a while before he finds out and goes berserk."

"And we finish what we started?"

"Yes, son, just like we talked about. Now, keep the tires on the road while your old man gets some shuteye."

"You bet, Pa. Shouldn't be too long now."

The Beast bounces up and down over uneven roads. It's becoming like a sauna under the blankets, so I peel a piece of the fabric off my face to breathe. We're surrounded by thick jungle trees with vines drooping from their branches like giant spaghetti noodles. *Did the doctor say Nicaragua? Jesus, we're in Central fuckin' America!*

My mind begins to creep into the dark zone. How are Chuck and Carter doing? Did they make it out of Snake Bend or are they dead from radiation poisoning? Fuck! My mother—she's with Jim—Junior is ten feet from us, that ogre who once tried to dismember me with an electric saw—thousands of essentials! I'm going to fucking die in the middle of a jungle!

Sunshine sets her hand on my knee. She

mouths: It will be okay. I nod and take a deep breath. *Shouldn't be too long now.*

The doctor snores for the rest of the drive, and Sunshine and I stay motionless in the back while wedged between us, Crutch keeps quietly fiddling with the controller. My legs cramp up and I'm sweating buckets under the blanket, but I don't dare make a sound.

Finally, the Beast comes to a stop. Junior wakes Doc and they climb out, slamming the doors behind them. I throw the blanket off our heads and watch them walk away. Holy shit—we're in the clear.

I scramble toward the perforated wall. Outside, the sun has begun to rise. I spot the painted buses a short distance away, now empty and parked single file, nose to bumper. Farther away, thousands of essentials are gathered on a field before a massive mansion. The structure looms against the backdrop of a jungle-covered mountain, its snow-white marble gleaming in the early morning light. From the front of the mansion, a terrace extends into the crowd like a stage.

The essentials could be mistaken for a concert audience waiting for the headliner to prance onstage, were they not so silent and still. Sunshine comes up next to me and takes in our new surroundings.

Far out to our right are rolling hills, where workers dotted among lush green rows of plants toil with farming tools. Their worn-out straw hats and dusty overalls suggest they've been here for a while, laboring under the sun and processing what look like coffee beans. Among them are a few men dressed in camouflage fatigues, with machetes strapped to their sides.

"This must be Holtz's coffee farm," I say.

"Not just coffee. Over there." Sunshine gestures to our left. "Look what they're doing."

A couple hundred yards away in that direction, the land abruptly falls away, blurring into the sky as if the world simply ends there. Near that edge, farm workers process stacks of long blade-like leaves. We watch as they slice the leaves in half with knives, scoop out their innards, toss the goo into a barrel, then fling the discards over the cliff's edge.

"Aloe vera," Sunshine says under her breath.

My attention snaps to movement on the mansion's terrace—Jim struts into view with a huge grin, waving his hands above his head like he's some kind of celebrity. The entire Holtz family follows behind him. But where is *she*?

Then my mother appears and strides to Jim's

side. He takes her hand in his—*that fucker*—and pulls a microphone from his jacket. He taps the mic, and a thud reverberates across the field. "Can you hear me out there?" he asks, his voice magnified by unseen speakers.

The essentials below him roar in unison, "We hear you, Father!"

Father?

"Fan-fuckin'-tastic! Look around you! Where are you now?" Jim cries.

"Paradise! Paradise! Paradise!" The essentials scream.

"Isn't it beautiful? We promised you paradise, and you see how we have made good on our promise, myself and Samantha!" Jim shouts, raising my mother's hand up high.

The essentials chant, "SAMANTHA! SAMANTHA!"

Samantha? My chest tightens. I think I'm going to be sick. What do I do now? My mind's racing, but it's coming up short.

You can't figure it out, Max, and you never will!! You'll end up six feet under like the rest of them and there's nothing you can do about it you miserable pathetic—

"Got it!" Crutch cries out.

I turn around. Crutch is beaming at me with the transmitter in one hand and the Playstation controller in the other. "It's ready?"

Crutch extends the antenna from the transmitter with his teeth. "Let's find out, Max."

"Hang on. I'm gonna get us closer to my mom. When I say go, Crutch, hit it." Before they can respond, I dart out the Beast's rear doors. As soon as I step outside, the heat hits me like a slap in the face with a wet towel.

I rip open the driver's-side door and see that the key is still in the ignition. For the first time in way too fucking long, I plop my ass on the Beast's worn leather seat like a foot into a well-worn shoe. Ah, baby, I've missed you.

The passenger door opens, and Sunshine jumps into the shotgun seat. "I'll be your lookout," she tells me.

I nod. Just then, another voice booms across the field.

"Hello, my essentials! Welcome to paradise!"

I look up to see Holtz front and center on the terrace, the mic held close to his lips. The crowd doesn't respond. Off to my right, I notice the folks with the machetes making their way toward the mansion.

Holtz continues. "We have traveled thousands of miles, and now we are finally here! But we don't have time to celebrate! Soon, the sky itself will betray us, but we will not wait for death to claim us! While the world panics, we shall rise, and your hands will forge the last vessel of mankind—a ship that will carry the chosen beyond the stars! You will build! You will fight! And together we will survive! Now, say it with me! You will build!"

But the essentials stay dead silent. What the hell is Holtz babbling about? Sunshine throws me a wild-eyed glance.

Holtz shakes his head in disgust as he hands the microphone to Jim. They seem to be talking to each other, but I can't hear a thing; I have to read their body language. From here, Jim looks confused, while Holtz looks firm, as if he's saying, "Do it, goddamnit, or else!"

Jim brings the mic to his mouth and says, "Essentials, you heard the man! You will build, you will fight, and we will survive!"

The essentials roar, "We will build! We will fight! We will survive! Survive! Survive!"

"I can't hear you!" Jim yells. "Tell me what you're going to do!"

"WE WILL BUILD, FATHER! WE WILL FIGHT, FATHER! WE WILL SURVIVE!"

Fuck this concert from the nosebleed section— time to crash the backstage. I twist the Beast's key and her V8 fires up with a throaty roar. My baby is alive, and I'm the one behind her wheel again!

"Guys, hold on!"

The Beast lunges forward. I steer her toward the line of parked buses and drive behind them, the buses acting like massive shields between us and the roaring crowd of essentials.

"What will you do?" Jim's high-pitched voice blares from the speakers.

"BUILD! FIGHT! SURVIVE!"

I keep my eyes locked ahead as we edge closer to the mansion. The Beast rumbles past the final bus, and now our shields are gone. We're exposed, but yet undetected. We're alongside the mansion now, closer than ever to my mother.

"Hit it, Crutch!" I yell.

"Copy that!"

I turn and see Crutch behind me, mashing on the Playstation buttons just like he did when playing Contra back at Chuck's house.

I return my gaze forward. The crowd of essentials all jump into the air at the same time. As they land, each kicks out a leg or throws out a punch that lands on their neighbors. The scene swiftly devolves into a frenzy of orchestrated violence that I can't help but watch in awe.

"Stop!" Jim cries out, and for a moment, the essentials settle. But Crutch hammers away again at the controller, and the bloody battle resumes.

The essentials collide together with sickening thuds, their fists pummeling, nails clawing, all blending into a nightmarish mosh pit that would make a Slayer concert look like a middle school dance. I see a man with wild eyes grabs a woman by the hair, yanking so hard that a chunk of her scalp rips away. She retaliates by sinking her teeth into his arm, savagely tearing flesh from bone.

I watch as another man claws at an older man's face, his nails leaving deep, bloody gashes. The older man responds by wrapping his hands around the other's neck and squeezing until his eyes pop like a squeezed zit. Before he has time to even release his victim, another essential's fist drives through his skull, exploding his brain and bone like a cannonball from the shattered crown.

"I COMMAND YOU TO STOP!" Jim screams. The essentials pay as little attention to him as they did Holtz.

Heads are rolling, literally. The essentials breach the terrace and everyone onstage flees except for Jim, my mother, and Louise Holtz, who looks frozen from shock. Three essentials surround the former governor, and two latch on to her arms. Simultaneously, they yank so hard that her arms rip from her torso. She screams until the third essential grabs her by the ears and twists her head off. Her body slumps to the floor, spouting fountains of blood.

"Keep it up, Crutch!" Sunshine exclaims. "I think you're about to get the high score!"

Jim and my mother are backing away from the essentials. Jim keeps yelling for them to stop, to no avail. There are now more essentials face-down than standing. Blood spatters the ground, turning the grassy field into a muddy, crimson mess.

An acrid stench of burnt plastic hits me. I twist in my seat to see Crutch smacking the transmitter. "It's burning up!" he yells. Smoke engulfs the rear. Crutch climbs out the back and tosses the smoking transmitter into the bloody field.

"You!" Jim screams into the mic. "STOP I SAY! ESSENTIALS, SURROUND THAT GINGER!"

A half-dozen essentials break apart from the rest to form a circle around Crutch. He tries to escape, but it's impossible.

"Simon," Jim hisses, eyeballing Crutch. "I should have known, my double-crossing nephew!"

Nephew?

"You're just like your father, and you're going to end up pushing daisies just like him and your brothers! Your bullshit games are finished! You see this mess you've made! You're cleaning it up, just like you did in the fucking pit! My children, bring him to me!"

The essentials hoist Crutch above their heads, carrying him away like a sacrifice. I lunge for my door, ready to chase after him.

"Holy shit, Max!" Sunshine screams. "What the hell is that?"

I freeze, and a grisly horror show unfolds before me. Chunks of torn flesh are slithering on the ground toward one another, snapping together like magnets wherever they meet. Tendons stretch and twist, bridging the gaps between severed arms, legs, and torsos.

Sunshine and I watch, paralyzed, as the limbs reassemble—not into their original forms, but into something grotesque and terribly wrong. Arms connect where legs should be, and hands sprout from chests; the bodies stitch together like a demented child's drawings, so disturbing it's painful to look at.

A voice in my head screams: *DRIVE!*

"Hold on!" I shout. I turn the wheel, aim straight for the monstrous mass between us and my mother, and slam the gas pedal to the floor. The Beast plows into the deformed essentials, their blood splattering against the windshield. Bones break, sounding like tree branches snapping under pressure. My gaze locks on Jim, who's still on the terrace with my mother.

His eyes widen in terror and recognition. "Samantha! Stop my meat wagon!" Jim screams, his voice crackling through the valley.

My mother stares at me intensely. She raises her hands and points them down toward us, and suddenly, the Beast screeches to a stop. I double-pump the gas pedal, but nothing happens. Why isn't she responding?

My mother and Jim step down from the terrace, side by side. "Maxwell!" Jim greets me with a snarl as they approach us, stepping over twitching body parts.

"Max!" Sunshine yells. "Drive us out of here!"

"I'm trying, but something's got a hold of my Beast!" I try to restart the engine, but the key won't turn, and the gas pedal is still doing jack shit.

"Bring them to me, my love!" Jim orders.

My mother moves so fast that she's a blur, only re-appearing when she has the door on my side torn from its hinges. She hurls the chunk of metal far into the field as if it weighs nothing, then she grips my bicep with hands like iron claws and yanks me out of the Beast. She reaches in and seizes Sunshine too, drags her out, then frog-marches us toward Jim.

Jim says, "Well, well, look who we have here. Stowaways!" He reaches out and squeezes my cheeks. My lips are forced together, fish-like.

Jim shakes his head, then stares out at the bloody field, then back to me. "I'm so, so disappointed in you, Maxwell. Your mother and I are deeply ashamed of your little rescue bullshit stunt you pulled. Aren't we, dear?"

"Ashamed indeed, Jim," my mother says in Samantha's voice. Jim squeezes my cheeks harder. My jaws ache. I try to speak, but only an incoherent grunt escapes.

"What was that?" Jim asks. "Are you trying to beg for your life, Maxwell? You want to join my circle of trust this time? You and your little girlfriend? She and I had so much fun together before, didn't we?" He jerks his hand up and down, forcing me to nod.

"Fuck you!" I spit out.

"Yeah, fuck you and your circle jerk!" Sunshine adds.

Jim releases my cheeks and slaps me across the face, hard. My head whips back—I see stars.

"You're not worthy of my circle, Maxwell. Neither of you. You're going to pay dearly for what you've done. Samantha, show them the lovely view, dear."

My mother forces us forward so incredibly fast that for an instant, the world warps like a psychedelic trip. The hazy dawn sky snaps into streaked ribbons of color, twisting like smeared paint across a canvas. The trees, the mansion, the field—it all stretches into ghostly streaks. I can't feel my body, can't tell if we're falling, flying, or dissolving into the air itself.

And then—the world slams back into focus, and I realize—we're at the cliff's edge. My mother releases us. We hit the ground hard on our bellies and struggle to catch our breaths. I glance over the edge, then wish I hadn't—a river churns violently at the bottom of the canyon far, far below. It gives me instant vertigo, and I turn my head from the sight. Over my shoulder, beyond my mother, I see Jim walking toward us, followed by a wall of essentials. There's no way out this time.

"Sunshine, this is all my fault. I'm so sorry. I should never have brought you into this."

"No sorries, Max," Sunshine replies, reaching for my hand. "This is where I'm meant to be." She squeezes my fingers tightly, and I squeeze back.

Jim's grating voice cuts in. "Ah! Look at these lovebirds."

We release our hands and roll over to face him.

"You two better sing your final song before you fly! Ha!" Jim cries gleefully. "Samantha, be a doll and throw out the trash!"

Sunshine and I are abruptly tossed into the air like a child's rag-doll toys. With one hand on each of our midsections, my mother has hoisted us straight up above her head. Her hair whips in the wind, and that's when I see it—a box and copper wires attached to the back of her neck, labeled *SAMANTHA* 1.0.

"Don't do this!" I plead, limbs flailing helplessly in the air. "Your name isn't Samantha! It's Anne Maddison!"

Her grip tightens painfully on my gut, and I let out a strangled scream.

"Too bad, Maxwell," Jim sneers. "You were invited into my circle of trust, but you fucked it up."

Circle of trust ... *circle*—a desperate idea strikes me. I reach into my fifth pocket, fingers scrabbling until they find my mother's wedding ring. I pull it out and thrust it down desperately toward my mother. "Mom, don't you remember this? You were married once! To my father! I'm your only son!"

"Aww, listen to that!" Jim laughs. "Maxwell is trying to have a heart-warming moment with his mother. What a fool! Samantha doesn't give a fuck about you!"

My fingers shake, but I paw at my mother's hand where it's clutching my ribs and peel back her ring finger. I shove the wedding ring home.

A moment later, the crushing pressure on my stomach lightens. "Max?" she whispers, her gaze softening as she stares up at the ring, then at my face.

"Yes, Mom! It's me, Max!" I gasp. "Your name is Anne Maddison, and I'm your son!"

"Max?" she murmurs again. She lowers us

gently to the ground. Sunshine wheezes beside me, clutching her belly.

"What the hell are you doing, Samantha?" Jim demands. "Get rid of them, now!"

"I can't," my mother says softly, rubbing her wedding band. "He's my son." She sounds like her old self again, the voice I've known all my life.

Jim's face twists with rage. "What? That spawn of yours is nothing but a useless wretch! We don't need him! Finish them both off and I'll give you a new child—a stronger, smarter child! Not this sniveling waste of—what's that?"

Jim lunges forward and seizes her wrist. With a violent jerk, he rips the ring from her finger. "Samantha, do as I say!"

My mother breathes in sharply. Her voice again altered, she says, "Yes, Jim ... as you wish."

Jim grins. "Fan-fuckin'-tastic!" He plants a sloppy kiss on my mother's cheek. "Too bad, Max. You won't be around to see your little sibling grow up."

He turns to Sunshine. "Oh, hi sweetheart," he coos. "You know what? I'll give you a choice, since you did such a great job making all that aloe medicine for me and my essentials—"

Before he can finish, Sunshine launches at him like a spider monkey. Her legs clamp around Jim's torso and her fists blur, beating his face like a drum. "You bastard!" Sunshine shrieks. "I'd rather die than ever work for you again!"

"MY CHILDREN!" Jim screams between blows. "GET THIS SKINNY BITCH OFF ME!"

I lunge to help Sunshine, but I'm too slow and his essentials are too fast. They peel her off their master and toss her to the ground. I rush to shield her with my body as she scrambles to her feet.

Jim laughs, spitting blood and a chunk of ivory from his mouth. "You two really are stupid. You deserve each other. Don't you see? This is my fucking kingdom. I'm in control. These essentials are mine! And your mother and I rule here as King and Queen!"

"Don't listen to him, mom! Listen to me!" I plead.

"Save your breath, Maxwell," Jim sneers. "You're not talking your way out of this."

"Mo—"

BAM!

Jim blindsides me with a brutal kick, sending me flying backward into Sunshine, and the ground drops out beneath us.

I look up and see the cliff's edge above me, with my mother and Jim peering over it. Jim with his fucking grin—now missing a front tooth—and my mother with her stone-cold gaze.

Sunshine and I plummet toward the river

below. This is it! You, me, all of them! We're all going to end up—Sunshine grabs my waist.

"Big breath!" she says.

I fill my lungs with as much air as they can hold. Sunshine's lips press against mine. The world falls silent—only to shatter when our bodies collide with the water.

Splash!

Acknowledgments

First and foremost, to my editors—without you, I'd be drowning in a sea of misplaced commas, and worse.

Minae Lee: from the depths of my heart, thank you for your patience as you navigate through my madness.

Sharon Stogner: thanks for giving it to me straight and on time.

A bittersweet thank you to the evil-minded assholes of the world: without you, life might just become a daytime rom-com re-run—boring.

And last but not least, to the readers, the book clubs, podcasts, and lit community across the web: your unrelenting hunger for more means everything.

I hope you enjoy reading *The Nonessentials II* as much as I did writing it.

– Zachary

Also by Z. Martin Brown

The Nonessentials (book one)

AVAILABLE AT:

VILLAGE BOOKS & PAPER DREAMS

BARNES & NOBLE

AMAZON

PATHOGEN PRESS

About the Author

Zachary worked in the film industry until the pandemic, during which he moved corpses for a mortuary. He currently lives in Arizona with his sweetheart, where he's creating extraordinary nonsense from inside air-controlled spaces. Contact him at www.zacharymartinbrown.com

www.ingramcontent.com/pod-product-compliance
Lightning Source LLC
Chambersburg PA
CBHW020132310726
48970CB00006B/1841